LOVE ME
TO
THE END

By

Justin Ekor

Love Me to the End

Author: Justin Ekor
Book Title: Love Me to The End
© Justin Ekor 2013
ISBN 978- 9988-1-8679-1

For Bulk Purchase, please contact:
Archbishop Amissah Memorial School
Box UC 163
University Post Office
Cape Coast
GHANA, West Africa
+233243268937/ +233202321218
justinekor6@gmail.com

Table of Contents:

Chapter One

Middle School Leaving Certificate Examination (MSLCE) results were released. Apati had a wind of the news the previous day. He went to his friend's house to let him know about the outcome. Nevertheless, Abrokwa heard the news but could not gather enough courage to go and verify what was written against his name: John Kuma Abrokwa. Distinction, Pass or Fail were the three options.

Abrokwa developed mixed feelings of fear and optimism. "After all, there are many who failed the examination during the previous years and are still enjoying life in the village as if nothing had ever happened to them," Abrokwa fortified himself. But there was one thing that was obvious. Those who had the red certificate – distinction, during the previous years were honoured by the elite of the village. These renowned citizens resided in Ho, Kumasi, Accra and elsewhere. Those who had ordinary passes were equally happy, though not honoured. Those who failed had no recognition from both young and elderly people of the village. People saw them as dregs of society. These were the thoughts that mumbled Abrokwa's cranium until he gave in to sleep.

Abrokwa did not wake up before Apati knocked on his door at dawn. Abrokwa was not happy when he saw Apati's face. Not happy because he was sure Apati would raise the results' issue and suggest that they should go to Mr Blizek for the outcome. Some say the day of writing an examination is uneasy but watching one's examination results is more terrifying. It takes the heart of a valiant person to walk in freely for an examination results. That was where Abrokwa's problem was.

"Abrokwa, Abrokwa, you are lucky! Lucky for you to sleep and snore over a mass failure," Apati spoke with disappointment.

"So far, all our friends who went for their results have failed miserably. And here you are still in bed, as if you have nothing to think about," Apati spoke again; now offensively.

This story forced Abrokwa out of his last dawn dreams. He stretched himself, wiped his face with his dirty cover cloth and asked hastily: "Did Collins go?"

"You don't know what is happening! Collins was the first to go because he trusted himself so much," Apati rumbled.

"And what was the outcome?" Abrokwa asked with heightened anxiety.

"It was a disaster!" Apati responded in a rather sad, low tone.

"What do you mean by the word disaster?" Abrokwa asked back.

"He failed!"

"You don't mean it, be serious, boy, and set jokes aside!"
"Have I ever deceived you?"
"Eh, fresh, green trees are burning! If the evergreen ones are burning this way, then what is going to happen to the old dry ones like me? This story won't be a good one to narrate. Could it be a curse or a plague?" Abrokwa squealed.

The news of the failure of Collins Apedo confused Abrokwa the more. He knew very well that if Collins should fail, then there was no hope for him. No hope for him because Collins was far better than him in class.

At this point, Abrokwa saw that the best way to solve the problem was to go and watch the results. Although he perceived his failure in advance, he believed in the adage that 'seeing is believing.' He that is down, fears no fall. It was the slaughtered goat who said he was already lying flat for the butcher's sharp knife. After all, the stone in a river does not fear cold.

Apati realised the level of restlessness running through Abrokwa's nervous system. He told him to stop disturbing himself over the examination results with unqualified speculations. Abrokwa then gathered courage to stop Apati from what he was saying about the results all that while. It could be true; it could be false. Abrokwa vowed not to ask Apati any question again. "After all, we don't guess in the presence of a fortuneteller. Let's go to the headteacher to see for ourselves what our fate is. Wonders happened before, and they can still happen. I believe in this. I do not believe in inferences. Until I see the results with my naked eyes, I won't believe anything thereof. You can call me doubting Thomas, I don't care!" That was Abrokwa.

"Do not talk again boy. Let's go there and see things for ourselves with our organs of sight. A valiant person never tastes of death but once. Soldiers go to war and return home safely. Let's go now," the two agreed and set off to Mr Blizek's house that morning.

Immediately Mr Blizek met Abrokwa and Apati, he shook hands with them and congratulated them on a good job done. The boys were surprised and got puzzled about the headteacher's actions. "This is a sarcastic action purposed to mock at us," they reasoned concurrently.

Mr Blizek led them to the school. He opened his office and beckoned them in. They walked timidly like mice and entered. They were given a long list of the results to go through. It was really disastrous. 'Fails' were lined up on the paper as if they were on parade. Apati saw his name and shouted on top of his voice – Distinction! Abrokwa's name was yet to be located. His heart trembled seriously and the paper dropped from his grips. All this while, Apati ran out of the room jubilating outside.

Mr Blizek identified Abrokwa's predicament. He tapped his back and encouraged him to have patience. He collected the results from the floor; located Abrokwa's name and pointed his pen to the remark – Distinction. Abrokwa was dumbfounded. He embraced Mr Blizek and hysterically ran out of the office to meet Apati with the outcome. The two boys sang loudly, jumped and shed tears of joys. Although most of their mates including Collins failed, Abrokwa and Apati   passed with distinction. There was no doubt about that.

Apati and Abrokwa's light began to shine gradually. At the end of that day, their lights shone brightly in all corners of the village. Boys feared them, whilst girls admired them. The news of their success spread like wildfire. People, both young and old visited them at home to congratulate them on their gallant victory.

Mr Blizek also visited Apati and Abrokwa at home to congratulate them. He told them that he was not surprised about their success and Collins' failure. According to him, what brought Collins down was pride and complacency. "Collins thought he was intelligent, therefore, he refused to respect teachers and colleagues. His pride pulled him down. He would learn a lesson from his failure if he is wise," Mr Blizek reiterated.

Mr Blizek reminded Abrokwa and Apati that in the contrast, their humility, obedience, respect for teachers and above all, their hard work was what accorded them their victory. He once again shook hands with them and praised them: "Congratulations! Your humility and hard work paid off."

Now, all the candidates who had distinction in all the ten communities of Kedam traditional area were honoured by the paramount chief in a grand style. A month later, members of the Kedam Development Association resident in Ho, Kumasi and Accra took their turn to honour the praiseworthy boys and girls. A week later, the parents of Abrokwa and Apati threw a party to bestow honour upon their children who made them stand tall among their colleagues.

During the ceremony, many ladies and gentlemen were invited. It was a gracious ceremony, therefore, even those who were not invited attended. Among those present was Sefakor, a form two pupil of Owle Local Authority Middle School.

Sefakor was a nice-looking, promising, young girl by all standards. Abrokwa caught a glimpse of the young school girl during the ceremony. He wanted to dance with her out of ecstasy but Sefakor declined and fled home immediately. She was shy and firm, therefore, would not allow anybody to see her with a boy in public; let alone dancing with a hero that all eyes were following at that moment. Of course, Abrokwa's demand embarrassed her so much that she quickly left for home.

Abrokwa became mortified by Sefakor's reaction to his application. He feared he would be teased and mocked at by his friends who saw clearly what cropped up between him and the fine young girl. It was something Abrokwa had never tried in his life but on that day, his victory and the ceremony in his honour gave him the guts to take that bold but fruitless stride. In fact, the encounter with Sefakor did not end Abrokwa's day well. Abrokwa was depressed and could not enjoy the rest of the ceremony as Apati did. He wished the girl never showed up at the ceremony at all. But that was not the solution. The two friends would have ended the day memorably if Abrokwa's head was not over swollen.

After the ceremony, everybody left for their homes. At dusk, after evening meals, every household conspicuously recounted the boys' performance. Many serious parents and guardians admonished their children and wards to follow the footsteps of Apati and his friend, Abrokwa. They had a good friendship, which led to great success. This was the kind of union discerning young and old people admired in the village. It was a good example from these young pals for others to emulate.

Chapter Two

By twelve midnight, the day and its activities were completely buried by Mother Nature. Only bats and crickets could be heard cheering from fields and tree-tops. The cries of giant owls could equally be heard far from thick forests. Men and women were dead in their beds; giving the chance for these and other nocturnal creatures to take over the ruling of the earth.

The next day rolled in with its activities. Abrokwa thought the previous day was gone with its troubles. Unfortunately, the hideous night that separated the previous day from the present one could not erode human memories. Some people could still recount Abrokwa's attempted encounter with Sefakor.

The first person who questioned Abrokwa about what happened between him and Sefakor was his bosom friend, Apati. Abrokwa could not tell the plain truth.

"That teenage girl wanted to dance with me and I refused. She became ashamed and left the party prematurely. Her untimely departure actually riled me." Abrokwa threw dust into his friend's eyes but the dust refused to settle.

"You are a hypocrite! A great liar! You cannot throw dust into my closed eyes. I saw and heard it all," Apati affirmed.

"You passed your examination and you thought that was the end of life. You wanted to seek a girl's hand in marriage openly. Even not in secret, but in the full glare of the whole village. *Abowa, kwasea, avukoklo*," Apati slurred and pulled Abrokwa's legs without compassion.

Apati lied to Abrokwa that his parents had lost hope in him for doing such a thing in their presence.

The utterances of Apati sent fears and uncertainty through the spine of Abrokwa. The comments from his friend made him more mystified. Abrokwa wept uncontrollably and vowed never to get close to any girl again in the village until his father performed the gun ceremony to usher him into adulthood. That would give him the audacity to approach a girl he loved publicly. Without that custom, it was an abomination for a boy of Abrokwa's age to do what he tried and failed. Abrokwa was wrong – totally wrong by moral standards of Owle. Abrokwa was lucky the girl did not duck to his whims. That would have caused him his fame in the village.

One Sunday morning, Abrokwa just came out from his house and entered a winding alley. He was on his way to a friend's house. He unexpectedly bumped into a girl on the narrow alleyway. This girl was no other girl than Sefakor Atipo. Sefakor was on her way to Sunday school. She looked gorgeous and splendid in her white church attire. She had her hair plaited beautifully with an impressive, sparkling, black thread popularly called *dablaka*. Sefakor's mother bought this beautiful *dablaka* from Obane market, purposely for her only daughter.

Spontaneously, the four eyes jammed, compelling both Abrokwa and Sefakor to arrest their footsteps abruptly.

Sefakor's heart quivered and her legs wobbled like those of a frustrated school teacher's conked out table. Abrokwa got totally confused and did not know what to do next. He wanted to greet but his throat got choked with words. His mouth ran out of saliva. Before he could finish saying good, and get to morning, Sefakor vanished into thin air.

Sefakor ran as if she had met a dangerous snake in the bush, which was pursuing her and she was running for her life. It was the Kedam lame man who vowed, he would also run very fast if he should see death coming.

Sefakor could not stop on the way until she reached home. She went home panting and sweating profusely. Her mother asked her what the matter was. She could not tell the truth.

"*Nene*, a snake, a very long one, the poisonous, black one called the cobra," she feigned. The mother inquired of where she met the dangerous snake that Sunday morning so the father would go and kill it. Regrettably, Sefakor could not tell the exact place that she met the phony snake. Rather, jokingly, she pointed a finger to a far away place where nobody could trace. This waned the interest of Sefakor's mother in the case.

Sefakor could not go to church again on that day because she met Abrokwa on the way. Frankly speaking, Abrokwa did not intend to ask Sefakor any question. Neither was he prepared to engage her in any conversation. That was far from it. Should he have the opportunity at all, he would only ask her for the reason why she disgraced him on that special day of his. Perhaps, Sefakor was not ready for any thing of that nature as well. She saw Abrokwa as someone who was tracking her and she wouldn't give him the least opportunity. The only remedy was to escape from the snares of her aggressor.

By Sefakor's action, Abrokwa could not go to his friend's house again. He returned home bewildered. Abrokwa pondered over his second encounter with Sefakor for the rest of the day and beyond. In the night Sefakor occupied Abrokwa's dreams from A to Z. In his first dream, he made a love proposal to Sefakor and she agreed, on condition that he would love her to the end of her life. Abrokwa was of the same mind and agreed to this fine condition. They then started making arrangements to meet somewhere to plan the marriage ceremony. Unfortunately, the meeting could not come off before Abrokwa woke up from his dream.

The following morning Abrokwa's spirit was filled with the fondest love for the inaccessible Sefakor. He now planned to take advantage of any meeting with her to tell it to her face. He would tell her about his deep affection for her and his desire to marry her one day when they both grow up. This decision was taken and settled on, but meeting Sefakor alone was a vision, which was hard to materialise. Sefakor did all she could to avoid Abrokwa whenever the chance seemed to come

Abrokwa's way. This made Abrokwa's desires remain in him and got enlarged like a notorious boil.

The bird learned to fly without perching on a twig, as the hunter learned to shoot without missing the target. When the bird makes the mistake to perch, the hunter will certainly finish it off. But, can the bird fly all day without perching on a twig as the hunter continues tracking it? The bird may not perch now! Would the hunter however not get tired of tracking it all day long? This was the mystical tale which confronted the two personalities in the picture. Sefakor was the bird and Abrokwa the hunter. Abrokwa would like to meet Sefakor by hook or by crook but Sefakor would not give him that opportunity. Certainly, the one who would win this battle needed better strategies.

Abrokwa kept on waiting for his lingering tactics to catch up with Sefakor as days turned into weeks and weeks into months but all in vain.

At a point, Abrokwa started growing lean and could not contain the situation any longer. His predicament was analogous to that of a twelve-month old pregnancy, showing no sign of labour. Yes, a voracious romantic fire was burning in Abrokwa for Sefakor. He needed an immediate solution to his problem before it sent him to his grave. Elderly people do say, a lingering problem of this sort remaining in an individual's heart could rupture the body. They often suggest that the best way to solve such a problem is to purge it through the word of mouth. This clearly dawned on Abrokwa. Thus, he decided to discuss his real problem with his best pal, Apati.

Abrokwa went to Apati and raised the topic jokingly, but Apati reframed the story into a serious one. Apati told Abrokwa that he once eavesdropped into a conversation between Sefakor and Dzifa one afternoon. Dzifa was a very good friend of Sefakor. According to Apati, the girls were on their way to farm to fetch firewood when he met them. And from what he heard from the horse's own mouth, if his ears did not deceive him, then there was a lot of love in Sefakor's heart for Abrokwa. Just that she has been shy to meet him face to face.

Apati's submission sounded like hamattan whirlwind in Abrokwa's ears. Shocked with skepticism, Abrokwa accepted what Apati said with a grain of salt. He thought Apati wanted to pull his legs one more time. He, Abrokwa, would not budge to this kind of antiquated camouflage. He warned Apati to remain focused and not to count the tails when asked to count the mice. Nevertheless, Abrokwa expected nothing short of what Apati was telling him, whether true or false.

Apati's utterances rekindled Abrokwa's tough love for Sefakor, assuming that at least every cloud has a silver lining. He vowed to go all out to propose love to Sefakor. He told himself that eat and die is better than living with hunger. He critically considered the various options by which to draw Sefakor into his net. Raining gifts on Sefakor, compelling her to develop love for him, sending someone to her to inform her of his love for her or tracking her in an obscure corner to tell it all to her, were the three options.

Love Me to the End

The first attempt was a failure. Abrokwa gave two pens to Sefakor's best friend, Dzifa, to be given to Sefakor. When she sent the pens, Sefakor rejected them. Abrokwa was not perturbed by Sefakor's reaction. He learnt a rhyme at kindergarten that when your efforts prove a failure, try again. Abrokwa, therefore, tried the second option quickly. He sent one of his cousins, Afuata to Sefakor the following day to let Sefakor know about his intentions to marry her in future. Afuata made the attempt but failed. Sefakor rained insults on her and her kin boy, Abrokwa. She claimed they had a calculated plan to destroy her life.

"I am a minor; don't come to me with such a silly matter again. I assure you, your next shot will land you in my father's wrath," she threatened Abrokwa's cousin. Nothing bothered Afuata more than the threat of reporting the episode to Aongo, the old soldier.

Aongo had no front teeth in his mouth. The story about how Aongo lost his teeth was well known to all and sundry at Owle. When Aongo was in the army, he was sent on a peacekeeping mission at Abyssinia in 1961. That was where he fell in love with a Yaltopyaian girl. The girl's father warned Aongo to stop following his daughter but this fell on deaf ears. One day, Aongo visited the girl at home and took her out of the house. Right at the back of the building, Aongo started caressing and kissing the girl. A passerby saw what the soldier was doing. He was surprised at what the peacemaker was doing to the young girl. He went to the house and reported the case to the girl's father. The girl's father came out to see Aongo and her daughter in the act. This man was a very strong old police man. He went home for a strong truncheon. He disguised himself; crept like a hunter and got close to them. He skipped and hit Aongo's mouth with the stout stick. Aongo's mouth was badly damaged. This brought out all the front teeth off Aongo's mouth. All his front teeth fell off on the spot and could not be replaced.

Aongo was repatriated to his home country, Ghana, immediately the information reached the Military High Command. Aongo could not finish his mission in Ethiopia because of a girl. He however managed to collect the truncheon from the Ethiopian and brought it to Owle. The missing teeth in Aongo's mouth always reminded him of the incident.

Sefakor was Aongo's only daughter. From infancy, he used to protect her with the Ethiopian truncheon. He used it to stop boys who used to get closer to his daughter. As Sefakor grew older, Aongo became less tamed. He hated to receive reports of boys and men feasting their lustful eyes on his daughter's maturing, protruding buttocks; let alone firing at her with love proposals.

Afuata knew very well about all this. She was cocksure that she and Abrokwa would be in trouble if Sefakor should report the case to her father as she threatened. Certainly, Aongo would not tolerate that nonsense.

Afuata thus thought it wise to plead with Sefakor to forgive her, which she readily did. She promised not to do that to her again. Sefakor considered her plea and rescinded her decision to let the cat out of the bag to her father. Afuata thanked Sefakor and left for home with modest apprehension.

Later, Afuata went to Abrokwa and narrated to him the upshot of the errand she ran for him. She pent up her heartache by warning him not to dream about Sefakor any longer. She chastised Abrokwa and told him about the awful character of Aongo, Sefakor's father who some people considered to be an alert madman. She reminded Abrokwa of the old traditional Akan adage *"Wok4 aware a bisa,"* meaning before you enter a house to marry, ask of the family history.

Thinking all that she told Abrokwa was inadequate; Afuata continued by counselling Abrokwa that enough was enough.

"Forget about this girl called Sefakor if you want to live long to enjoy more birthdays in this world. It was the Kedame river which said: 'If I had someone to caution me, I wouldn't have fallen into the deep valley," Afuata reiterated sternly.

Abrokwa was greatly disappointed by all that he heard from Afuata but had nothing to say. He saw reason and agreed with all that Afuata said but dimly.

He promised to do everything within his ability not to think about Sefakor again. He thanked Afuata sincerely for her sisterly advice. And before anybody could see them to ask of what they were discussing, they both dispersed for their various homes.

Chapter Three

By six in the evening, the full moon appeared like a ball from behind the mountains. It was a good period for children to play along the major streets of the village. The young men bathed and sprayed their clothes with the latest high scented perfumes. Ladies did same with Saturday Night powder. Of course, everybody liked Saturday Night powder, which was popular among ladies in the village. They smeared the powder on their faces, armpits and elsewhere. The young men had ten or twenty pesewas on them for a tin of sardine, corned beef or Geisha tin fish. They went out of their houses with small Okapi knives to spend a good moonlit night. They would use the knives to open the tin fish. They would return to their places of abode around 10.00 pm to sleep for the rest of the night. Young girls who would not comport themselves during such a night were the loose ones destined for teenage pregnancy. They had high appetite for food and tin fish. The boys would take advantage of this weakness of theirs to lure them into their nets.

Boys who would not go out on the narrow streets would spend their full moon evening around their grandfathers to listen to old-time folktales.

Abrokwa was supposed to go out with his friends that night but for the first time, he did not. After the evening meal, he took his bath and sat on a flat stone at the entrance of the house quietly. Apati was at Abrokwa's house at twilight, well prepared for the night, but Abrokwa was not in a good mood. Apati asked Abrokwa what the problem was, but he said nothing tangible. "Abrokwa, is your mother dead?"Apati asked jokingly.

"Not at all, she is in the kitchen," Abrokwa replied. Apati then approached the kitchen and asked Abrokwa's mother of what Abrokwa's problem was.

"It was the Agbozume ghost that asked, 'Mahanya *na woa?*'" that was Abrokwa's mother. Comically, she started narrating the etymology of this popular Ewe adage to Apati.

"One day, a woman died in a town called Agbozume. The ghost of the woman was hurriedly leaving the town when some strangers coming to the town met it on the outskirts. The people heard the cries and wailing of the town folks. These people were crying bitterly when the carpenters were nailing the coffin of the dead woman. The strangers asked the woman they met about what was happening in the town for which the people were crying like that. Her reply was, "*Mahanya na woa* – do I know for them?"

Abrokwa's mother's story aroused some fear in Apati for listening to a story about a ghost that night. Obviously, Abrokwa's mother did not know about Abrokwa's problem and did not bother to ask because she was not interested. After all, Abrokwa was not sick. She gave him a bowl of *fufu* with delicious soup that evening and he ate it very well.

Apati saw that Abrokwa would not go out that night, therefore, he also left for home because the night would not be good for him without Abrokwa. Whatever Abrokwa's problem was, time would surely tell it to everybody.

The latest development regarding Sefakor dashed all hopes of Abrokwa. Abrokwa had no alternative than to jettison his unquenchable thirst for Sefakor. Actually, Abrokwa was among the four school boys that Aongo disciplined one day for climbing a coconut tree behind his house. From that day, Abrokwa feared Paa Aongo more than a wounded lion. Some say love is blind, perhaps, that was what made Abrokwa forget about what he suffered in the hands of Aongo, the ex-serviceman.

Abrokwa recounted the bitter experience he and his colleagues had from that old soldier. Impulsively, series of recollections that could help Abrokwa forget about Sefakor were invited by his conscience. He remembered his first encounter with Sefakor on the day of his honour, then how Sefakor used to flee whenever she saw him, as if he was a wild animal. All signals were clear to him that after all, Sefakor had no speck of space in her heart to accommodate him as falsely professed by Apati. It was now crystal clear to Abrokwa that he was fighting a vain battle, therefore, must recoil to his shell.

The trouble did not end there. The more Abrokwa tried to ignore Sefakor, the more his instincts reminded him about Sefakor's beauty and how important she would be in his life. He envisioned how he would walk abreast of Sefakor on Owle streets with pride.

Sefakor was really a pretty girl that many men in the village admired, including her teachers. What drove flies away from Sefakor, as if nobody liked her was her father's abhorrent temperament. This made her a free girl from the harassment of any man in the village. They all knew about Aongo's Ethiopian truncheon.

The teacher who hit Sefakor's buttocks with his palm before whipping her had a fair share of Aongo's bullies on that day. He did not understand why a teacher should take advantage of her daughter's offence and feast on her virgin buttocks. Perhaps, Abrokwa forgot about all these stories that surrounded the beautiful juvenile flower of the village, which he was poised to pick by hook or by crook.

One night, during a night vigil, Abrokwa and his friend Apati met Sefakor and her friends at the market place, where people gathered to dance *borborbor*. Throughout their stay, Abrokwa did not lift his hungry eyes from Sefakor. Sefakor who knew very well that Abrokwa was the only young man in the village who had the guts to propose love to her was also spotting Abrokwa but sporadically. Although they were a bit far from each other, their eyes met several times. Abrokwa got perplexed by this and wished he could approach Sefakor that night to tell her something but that was impracticable for him. Finally, he had no alternative than to get back home and throw his worried body on a scanty mat, which served as his bed.

Throughout the night Abrokwa dreamt about Sefakor again till daybreak. This time round, he decided to launch another onslaught on her; directly or indirectly.

"Aongo or no Aongo, I shall try my luck again! Sefakor will surely be my wife one day and me her husband. The valiant person never tastes of death but once, it is only cowards who die many times," Abrokwa flattered himself.

Abrokwa now decided to involve one of his parents in the rush. He thought it wise to discuss it first with his mother. She appeared to be more patient than his father. Secondly, she was interested in having grand children.

One early morning, Abrokwa went to his mother. "*Nene*, I have something very important to discuss with you," he told his mother.

"What is the matter, can I invite your father?" Abrokwa's mother asked.

Abrokwa said, no, he would like his father to be far from the issue. Abrokwa's mother then told Abrokwa to wait till evening before she could lend ear to his stuff. She perceived the issue to be a trivial one since Abrokwa would not like his father, the head of the family to be part of the meeting. Abrokwa told his mother that he could not wait till evening as the case was a pressing one to him. The mother then felt the urgency of Abrokwa's case. Perhaps, he wanted to discuss his plans of going to a secondary school to study Science, instead of the father's decision to make him learn a trade. This could be a pressing issue to address as time was running out. Already, most parents had finished buying things in their children's prospectus, whilst Abrokwa's father was still adamant.

The busy woman dragged a stool and sat down as she drew one closer to herself for Abrokwa to do same. She then in a low motherly tone asked Abrokwa to tell her his problem. Abrokwa did not know where to start. But before he could speak, his mother jumped the gun by asking Abrokwa how prepared he was to attend a boarding school. This question nearly swayed Abrokwa from the real message. But he controlled his composure and started.

"*Nene*, for some time now, an issue has been occupying my thoughts seriously. I would like to discuss it with you so that we see the way forward."

"My son, don't worry at all, I have been speaking with your father over this for some time now and he is trying to see reason."

"*Nene*, please relax and hear my story before you speak. One day, I was going to farm to fetch foodstuffs and I met a pretty girl on the way. Her appearance charmed me so much and I would like to marry her when I grow," Abrokwa broke the pot.

"You relax, I shall think about it and get back to you in a jiffy," that was Abrokwa's mother. "But do not let this be a bother to you as you are still a minor," she added.

Abrokwa's mother reminded Abrokwa that the two of his elder brothers were still there without wives, therefore, pushing Abrokwa's agenda ahead of theirs would be a matter of dancing before the drumbeat.

On one hand, Abrokwa's mother's decision to think about the matter and get back to him before long was welcomed by Abrokwa. On the other hand, her reference to his brothers as not yet married did not go down well with him. It was clear to him that the issue her mother raised could be a tangible hindrance on his way. It was a potential concern to dog his steps should the matter get to his father's chamber.

Abrokwa mitigated his uncertainties by thinking that should plan 'A' fail, there could be a plan 'B'.

Chapter Four

Misi Ghana be gbe ke yeku la,
Misi Ghana be gbe ke yeku la,
Misi Ghana be gbe ke yeku la,
Akpese vua nede gbe ne yease.

Right after this song, the big *kamasa* sounded loud and clear during the early part of dusk. All ears were anxious, awaiting the message that would follow. Definitely, the chief had a message for his people. And that was what the gong-gong beater was about to announce to the residents. Usually, when the town-crier sang before beating the gong-gong, it meant he had happy tidings for the people. But with the song about Miss Ghana, then there was no doubt that a marriage ceremony or puberty rite was in the offing. Surely, that was the announcement from the chief. Seven maidens from the seven clans of Owle were ripe for marriage and must be taken through this rite of passage.

Many people hailed the news with blissful clamour right after the first announcement. Many children gathered and followed the gong-gong beater throughout his assignment. They also sang the song with him before and after the sound of the gong-gong that preceded and the one that followed the last sound of the hollow, metal instrument. Like a snowball, the number of children increased from one place to another.

At first, the children were few when he made the first announcement in the mission community popularly known as Kpodzi. But before he could reach the downtown, there was a crowd of countless children following him. These children were mainly boys with few disobedient girls who would not stay home to help their mothers with the evening chores.

Seven days to the rice festival, the rite would take place. The crier was intoxicated, therefore, at certain areas he would stop for a moment to recollect some aspects of the message that he forgot. In that case, the children had to come in to remind him of the missing link before he could continue. There were some parts of the village where he would just send the message uncompleted. He would not end it because he could not remember the rest, leaving the audience in an overall suspense.

In fact, Abrokwa was very keen on listening to the whole message that evening but unfortunately for him, the worst thing happened when the town-crier reached Ayega clan – Abrokwa's community. After the gong-gong, the crier conveyed his message as if he was a chronic stammerer. He spoke with involuntary pulses and pale repetitions. His voice modulation was spongy. He could not finish the entire message and so the children could not sing the last song. They got confused about the turn of events and scattered. They shrank into oblivion one after the other like grasshoppers whose cassava tree on which they perched had been shaken. Thereafter, the children resurfaced at their various homes at the last moments of dusk.

Abrokwa's desire to get confirmation on the popular rumour about the puberty rites for the young girls landed on rocks. Nevertheless, the song about Miss Ghana made him guess a ceremony regarding the feminine sex was just round the corner. He wished he had heard it loud and clear from the horse's own mouth but that eluded him.

Exactly a week later, names of girls who were all set for the ceremony were established. Apati was the first among the young men in the village to unearth the names of the girls. He went to Abrokwa to ask him whether he was aware that Sefakor would partake in the rites. Apati was cocksure of the message but Abrokwa was a bit skeptical. The girls whose names were released were older in age than Sefakor. Secondly, he doubted who could convince the old soldier, Aongo, to allow his daughter to pass through an antiquated rite that would make men cast their lustful eyes on his daughter's partially naked body.

All families prepared their maidens very well for the custom. Three days to the rice festival, the rites were performed. Surely, Sefakor was among the selected maidens. She and her colleagues were beautifully dressed to the admiration of many people especially young men. As tradition demanded, they were bare-chested, exposing their succulent virgin breasts to public glare. The young men who had business there to accomplish were happy about what they saw. Many men confessed openly that

Sefakor's erect breasts and smooth thighs had the qualifications that could easily move a bishop out of a consecrated pulpit. Abrokwa stood by the roadside to observe the maidens. His eyes singled out Sefakor out of the rest of the young maidens. He glued his eyes on Sefakor's half-naked, adorned body and his thinking cap fell off his head. He spoke to himself aloud in public without knowing it. He declared openly that he would be the first man to propose love to Sefakor right after the ceremony. "Talk is cheap, try it and see what Aongo will do to you!" This was the comment one gentleman standing by threw at him after his artless declaration.

Chapter Five

The toils of the day had almost settled. People assessed and recounted their achievements and failures during the day. They tried to get resolutions for the days ahead of them.

It was this atmosphere that permitted Abrokwa to recall all the efforts he made to draw Sefakor into his web prior to the rites. He realised that all his labours yielded no benefits. Now he had settled on another formula – this time, with some academic dexterity. "The pen they say is mightier than the sword," he reminded himself.

"I will purge my passion on a white sheet of paper via ink to Sefakor and see the results," Abrokwa reflected.

Abrokwa studied a bit of literature at middle school. He knew very well that words that could have an influence on a reader or listener's mind must be carefully selected and arranged in a creative manner.

Throughout the night, Abrokwa reassessed his stubborn love for Sefakor. He thought seriously about the kind of language that could carry his strong emotions to the beautiful girl. Abrokwa had a sleepless night, rolling from one end of his mat to the other; pondering over what exactly to put on paper. He concluded that this should be a letter of similes and metaphors: a few onomatopoeias and hyperboles could serve as groundnut flavour. And some exaggeration would project real feelings that could tend a naïve female mind up side down.

At dawn, Abrokwa grabbed a ball pen and a writing pad to write. He drafted the first copy, edited it and produced the second edition. He then came out with the revised copy: proofread it, and then settled on the final copy.

> Yohanes E.P Church,
> P.O Box 12,
> Kedame Owle.
> 12th July, 1974.

Dear Sefakor,

How are you? I'm hopeful you are as fit as a fiddle. I'm full of thanks to the Almighty God that I've seen another brand-new day.

Sefakor, from the day I met you at my graduation ceremony, I've never been a free person.

In fact, I had a dream the previous night and I visited a beautiful, vast, flower garden. Earnestly speaking, there were a lot of strikingly, beautiful flowers in the garden. I was anxious to pick many but I was warned by the gardener to pick only one. I took my time and went round the whole garden. Finally, my eyes caught a glimpse of a fragrant, pretty one that was better than any other flower in the garden by all standards. It beckoned me gracefully and I approached it. Beaming with smiles, I drew closer to this flower and picked it with great pleasure. I was fully pleased deep down in my heart with everything about this flower. After a critical look at the whole bloom, I observed that an inscription was glittering on each of the petals. I carefully studied the writing and realised that it was a name therein and this name was Atipo Abla Sefakor.

My heart leaped out of the blue and I left the garden for home. You were the first person I met on my way home. Happily, I handed the flower over to you. You smiled at me and swiftly collected the flower from me. You were very pleased with this flower. That was not all; you hugged me and planted a charming kiss on my lips. The commanding taste of your tongue, in fact, landed me into a new world. In this new world, I met a host of angels described as angels of love. They revealed to me wonderful love tips, which I should exploit in making you feel at home whenever you fall into my arms.

When I woke up, I consciously narrated the dream to a renowned prophet. He interpreted the dream to me. According to him, it is destined from the genesis of life that you and I would be lovers and later become husband and wife in future.

Sister Sefakor, I cannot hide my feelings from you. Truly, I love you more than succulent honey harvested from a hard rock. Without you, life will be worthless for me. You are like a bright morning star on my path. When I set my eyes on you in the darkest part of the night, I see nothing but brilliant light. I find it difficult to comprehend the artistic fingers that created you. With you around me, I can live for weeks without food.

Earnestly speaking, there is no lady in this world that can move my heart the way you are doing to me. Darling, it is not your fault. Just accept to be my lover as it has been planned from the foundation of the universe and I will be healed from a protracted illness once and for all.

Sefakor, be kind enough to a poor in heart person like me and take a bold decision without hesitation. Do not look back at your father and shake your head in a pessimistic manner. Take a breath, smile, and nod in the affirmative and that would end all my troubles in this world.

Sefakor, you are the person who occupies my whole heart. You are solely my peace and comfort. In point of fact, it is sacredly accepted by all and sundry that paradise is a nice place. But I bet my bottom dollar that if it is because of you alone that I will miss the golden city of heaven, then I agree that my soul should remain on earth for ever and ever. How can I live and feel happy without your juicy lips, cute nose and succulent golden breasts?

Oh! I cannot imagine the kind of heaven I would find myself if you can just tell me that you love me as well.

Esefakor, gather courage and meet me at the primary school compound tonight. Just inform your parents that you are attending a Christian Youth Builders' (CYB) meeting, which most of the young ones in the village do patronise. There, I shall meet you and have a nice heart-to-heart chat with you. This will be a special tête-à-tête, which no one had ever had with you since you were born. I shall express my honey love to you through a fantastic gift, which I have prepared in a special way for you. Yes, my heart is dying for you.

Honey, I beg you; don't let anybody know about the content of this letter. No individual or group of persons should read it apart from you, my idol. Let this be a deep secret between only the two of us.

May the good Lord and guardian angels of love protect and guard you safely until we meet at the scheduled venue this evening at eight. Bye for now, and stay blessed!

Your darling boy,
Abrokwa.

The letter was well written, but getting it into the hands of Sefakor was the next hurdle to surmount.

Abrokwa sprayed the beautiful pieces of paper of the writing pad with Saturday night perfume. He wrapped the letter nicely, and gave it to his friend, Apati for onward transmission to Sefakor. He craved Apati's indulgence to make sure he did his best to give the letter to Sefakor by defying all possible odds.

The next day, early in the morning, Apati went and stood in a curve on the path that Sefakor used to take to school. At exactly 7:25am Apati pictured Sefakor emerging from a shrouded bliss from afar. He repositioned himself so that Sefakor would not see him before getting to the spot that he laid his ambush. When Sefakor was almost there, Apati pretended to have lost something vital, which he was busily looking for in the short grasses near the road. Luckily for him, Sefakor was walking alone before she got there. Sefakor's face met with that of Apati. She decided to have pity on him by helping him locate what he was looking for. Apati took advantage of Sefakor's kind gesture and quickly presented the letter to her as a gift from someone for her.

"Sefa, this is a gift from a friend of yours to you," he droned satisfactorily. Like a dawn charm, without any question, Sefakor took the letter, thanked Apati and hastily went her way. Apati grinned and bade Sefakor a fair farewell.

Chapter Six

A gentle wind blew and kissed the petals of flowers on top of the trees that lined up along the road. Two small colorful birds chirruped affectionately and flapped their wings concurrently. Sefakor felt the bliss of nature as the cold wind cuddled and patted her virtuous body to wipe off sweat from her face and armpits. She took a deep sigh and felt adoringly within herself.

This show of nature carried Sefakor's psyche away from what Apati gave to her. After a few minutes, she returned from that dreamland to her real world. She felt the letter on hand and she smartly dipped it into her school bag and continued her journey to school. She walked briskly to avoid the site of anybody that could see her collecting anything from a boy. That could brand her a spoilt girl in the eyes of the village. After taking a bend, where Apati would no longer see her, she started contemplating about what that gift could be. "What might this envelope contain?" questioned her conscience. She, however, disregarded any further fret over the envelope as the day was still young. She had to hurry up to school, tidy up her plot and sweep the classroom before the bell would be rung for assembly.

Sefakor finally decided on reaching home in the afternoon before opening the envelope to check up what it contained. But anxiety and apprehension set in, therefore, she decided to stop somewhere along the road for a brief moment to see exactly what the envelope contained. She pictured a shady tree ahead of her and targeted it to be the stop point. She hurried towards the tree. Unfortunately for her, on reaching the rest stop, some of her schoolmates who walked from far away villages were there resting on a fallen branch that created a bench for them. Sefakor's plans were dashed so she moved ahead. The presence of her schoolmates at the spot slowed down her anxiety but she couldn't control her agitations entirely. Spontaneously, she stopped somewhere and removed the envelope from her bag and opened it. She realised that it was a letter. Her feelings got churned up when the fragrance of the Saturday Night perfume caressed her nose. This coerced her to read the letter quickly.

She tried to glance through the letter at a very fast speed. Like the speed of a spacecraft, she read it from the beginning to the end. She folded it quickly and put it back into the bag. A quick idea came to her mind to shred the letter into pieces and throw it away. But something quickly whispered to her not to do so. Her sense of self also warned her that, that wasn't the best choice. A couple of thoughts rained within her mind from all possible angles. Her passions reminded her that there was no thorough decipher of the content of the letter due to the speed at which it was read. Of course, she needed another chance to read it again. After that she would decide on exactly what to do with it in order to nip in the bud any mess it was likely to bring her way.

It was now getting to 8:00 in the morning. Sefakor rushed to school, swept the classroom and tidied up her plot before the bell was rung for assembly. She was such a smart girl and many teachers admired her for her agility and brainpower.

In fact, some words and sentences in the letter caught Sefakor's attention and rang a bell in her heart. These words acted like the bait on a hook that a smart little fish cannot ignore, despite the lucid danger. Sefakor tried to sweep this pressure under the carpet and do a thorough reading of the letter secretly after school. That was a laudable decision but her ability to hold onto that was the impediment.

Sefakor's world began changing gradually. She was in a state of dilemma. She was afraid to take the letter home because she feared she would put herself into trouble should her father get hold of it. Sometimes that man behaved as if there were spirits working on him. Keeping such a secret from him was a difficult thing to do as the spirits could direct him to the letter once it entered his territory. Reading the letter at school and throwing it into the bush could be the best option. After all, if you can't run, you must know how to hide.

When the first lesson began, Sefakor tried to concentrate but all too soon, daydreams set in. Some invisible force was pushing her to read the letter now or never. This happened to her whilst the teacher was busy teaching. Then another thought crossed her mind. The idea was that some of her mates could see her and should the boys, especially, get hold of the letter, she could be reported to the teacher. That would be more serious than the old soldier getting hold of it. This really scared her and sent shivers down her spine. Owing to this, Sefakor did not make any attempt to read it till the end of the lesson. She forgot about it by force – for a while.

The letter's case became a problem in the mouth that the mind would like to ignore but the tongue cannot. The first lesson was over and the second one just began. It was time for Mathematics. Now Sefakor's mind was preoccupied with nothing but the lyrics of the love letter. She tried to control herself in order not to read it in the classroom but all attempts made to avert this temptation were a flash in the pan. She felt uneasy as if she was suffering from a protracted ailment that no medicine had a strong efficacy to cure. Sharply, a recalcitrant ego developed within her.

"After all, all die be die!" she thought.

She tilted her head back and forth, left and right to check if anybody's attention was on her. Nobody was looking at her. All attention was on the teacher who was then struggling with a long-division problem. Peacefully, she removed the letter from the bag; opened it and started reading it under cover. She read the whole letter but she was lucky that nobody saw her. She folded it back to its original place in the bag and heaved a deep sigh. Sefakor then became Alice in Wonderland. She took the letter again and started analysing it more carefully. This time around she got buried into it by its colourful flattering words. She forgot about herself. She forgot completely that she was in a classroom where a teacher was teaching. She then took a pen and wrote a footnote under the letter. This short note read: "Love me to the end: don't leave me on the way!"

Suddenly, Sefakor's indifference caught Mr Boso's attention. He quickly called her and posed a question to her. Sefakor got startled and quivered. It was the Kedam monkey which said that dropping from a tall tree is faster than climbing down. Sefakor dropped the letter rapidly and looked directly into her teacher's face. She tried to recollect the question to make an attempt to answer it but that was impossible. It was impossible for her because she did not hear the question well. Mr Boso was the type who would not repeat a question during lessons. Sefakor was very much aware of that therefore, she did not have the guts to let him repeat his question. She gazed at the teacher sheepishly, as confused as a cow on ice.

It was crystal clear to Mr Boso that Sefakor was not paying attention. He asked her to reproduce the last sentence of his lesson. Unfortunately for Sefakor, she could not reproduce a single word out of that group of words.

The hasty nature by which Sefakor sped the letter into her bag made the letter lose its way. It fell on the ground without Sefakor noticing it.

Mr Boso, who suspected that Sefakor was preoccupied by something else asked her to stand up. Now, the attention of the whole class was shifted from the cumbersome Mathematics lesson to Sefakor.

"Hey girl, what were you reading?" Mr Boso questioned Sefakor.

"Nothing sir," she replied.

Mr Boso was getting suspicious and livid. His eyes were very sharp despite his age. He saw a piece of paper under Sefakor's desk as he bent down to pick a piece of chalk, which fell from his table. He gradually moved towards Sefakor's place after picking the chalk. Before he could reach there, a colleague alerted Sefakor about her handkerchief lying on the floor. Sefakor got to know that it wasn't a handkerchief but rather the letter that lost its way and landed on the floor. She picked it up fast before Mr Boso got there.

Mr Boso asked Sefakor to give what she picked from the floor to him. Sefakor quickly gave to him another piece of paper, which she removed from her bag. Unfortunately, it was a blank A4 sheet of paper, which had nothing on it to decode. She wanted to play a fast one on her teacher but you cannot teach an old dog new tricks. Mr Boso had taught for several years and knew very well about pupils' funny tricks. Through experience, it was clear to him that Sefakor was out to outfox him. No, he would not succumb to this infant trick. He folded the piece of paper Sefakor gave to him and shredded it into pieces. He then took hold of Sefakor's bag and retrieved exactly what he saw on the floor. Sefakor sat quietly staring at what her teacher was doing, as if she had no business there. She did not utter a word nor made any attempt to collect the bag from the teacher.

First, she thought Mr Boso would just keep the letter somewhere without reading it. And later, he would punish her and give it back to her. That was what Mr Boso used to do to students who used to misbehave during lessons. But on that day, Sefakor's assumption was wrong – the story became a different one. Mr Boso quickly opened the letter and started reading it word for word, line by line. Within the twinkling of an eye, he read the whole epistle from A to Z. He nodded his head several times like a lizard on a broken wall timing a loose insect. He began again after the first reading, now more cautiously. Finally, he shook his head in utter surprise. Sefakor who looked outwardly unconcerned expected an insult from Mr Boso to end the whole episode. That expectation also did not materialise. Mr Boso threw a stern look at Sefakor and realised that she sat quietly unperturbed, as if she knew nothing about what was amiss. After the third reading, Mr Boso took the letter and left the classroom. Perhaps, he was going to put it into the waste paper basket. Sefakor now heaved a sigh of relief.

Chapter Seven

When Mr Boso left the classroom, he stood on the corridor for a while. After that he headed towards the headteacher's office.

At this time, Sefakor felt some heat transmitting through her spine at the speed of lightning. Her stomach rumbled and the colour of her eyes changed without prior notice. She knew her doom was at hand should that wicked headteacher have access to the letter. Sefakor got startled by the turn of events but gathered courage to watch Mr Boso through the window. She saw that he entered Mr Pataku's office and spent a few minutes there with him. Later, Mr Boso returned to the classroom without the letter.

Sefakor started hatching plans and strategies that she would use in defending herself if she should be asked to do so. "After all, I know nothing about the writer; someone just gave the letter to me. Is it a crime to be befriended by a boy who loves you?" she pondered.

Sefakor did not stop contemplating what would happen next before the bell was rung for assembly. It was a crisis call of pupils on an unusual hour of the day. What was really boiling in the pot on that odd hour did not catch any pupil's imagination. Now, all pupils from class one to middle school form four ran hither and thither and trooped to the assembly ground in fear and trembling. They lined up waiting quietly for critical information from the person who convened the meeting. They were summoned at exactly 10:55 am. Teachers did not have any firsthand information about the emergency forum, therefore, some of them hastened to the venue whilst others delayed.

Mr Pataku in his usual white long-sleeved shirt tacked in a black pair of trousers with big empty belt holes stepped forward and mentioned Sefakor's name with wrath. He commanded her to come forward and mount a table placed in front of the whole school. Only notorious boys used to mount that shameful table. Sefakor was not the type who breached school rules and regulations, therefore, the mention of her name caused mixed feelings among many teachers and pupils. The assembly ground became quiet and all eyes were glued on her.

All ears were hungry to hear of the exact offence that she had committed. Sefakor was shocked by this because she never expected things to go that way. In fact, she knew what was amiss so she became highly ashamed of herself. It was becoming very difficult for her to face the whole school. She was confused and did not know exactly where to turn her face to. Her legs wobbled under her as if they were tired of her posture and were no longer ready to perform their duties. Despite all these ordeals, she did not lose her composure.

Mr Pataku spoke with a stubborn, horrible voice. He announced that Sefakor broke one of the serious rules of the school and deserved a severe punishment. He went straight ahead to declare the offence.

"The offence this shameful girl committed was that she received a love letter from her boyfriend and brought the letter to school. She has no respect for me and the school authorities, therefore, she was reading the letter in the classroom whilst Mr Boso was teaching Mathematics. The letter was more important to her, hence, she was not interested in the lesson. What worsened her offence is that she deceived Mr Boso when asked to produce what she was reading by giving to him a blank sheet of paper. By this act, Sefakor by the laws of the Republic of Ghana, deceived a public officer on duty," he declared.

Mr Boso listened to Mr Pataku with keen interest. Mr Boso made interjections undertone to give support and authenticity to the charges leveled against Sefakor. When Mr Pataku was done, Mr Boso took over.

"The worst thing Sefakor did was that after reading the letter, she wrote under it 'Love Me to the End: don't leave me on the way.' This is something she cannot deny," he emphasized. "As if that was not enough, she insulted me; old teacher, Boso that I was a big fool upon trying to investigate from her the boy who wrote the despicable letter," Mr Boso garnished his comments treacherously.

Mr Boso took the letter and read it to the whole school carefully. There was an uproar from the entire school after they heard of the contents of the letter and the footnote which Sefakor scribbled under the controversial letter. Most of the big boys and girls from the school yelled: "Crucify her, kill her, she is a bad girl, this is unheard of in this school!"

The school children hooted and ridiculed Sefakor continually with contempt and derision, as if she was the worst criminal the school had ever seen.

"Bad girl, *ashawo*, prostitute," and many other insults were thrown at her like stones from a catapult being hurled at a heroic vulture. In fact, on that day, Sefakor had no friend in the school to sympathise with her except her younger brother, Daada, who was crying profusely all along. To be frank, the offence of the two boys who broke into the headteacher's office and made away with school fees and books was rather taken on a lighter note. Some female teachers complained about this sort of injustice against girls and women in this patriarchal society of ours.

"Order, order, silence, silence!" teachers shouted to control the hue and cry. They tried to maintain a firm atmosphere in order to pave the way for Mr Pataku to pronounce Sefakor's sentence. When the noise subsided, the headteacher spoke on: "The laws of this school do not allow the kind of behaviour Sefakor has put up, therefore, she will be punished ruthlessly," he fired.

Sefakor tried to defend herself but nobody was ready to listen to her. What bothered her was the lie that she insulted her teacher, which she did not do as a matter of fact. In point of fact, that allegation was what made her offence very severe to serious-minded   teachers and pupils.

To execute Sefakor's punishment, four strong boys were invited to stretch her on the table that she mounted. As if they were already hungry for a revenge match, they immediately stretched her on the table; each of them seizing one of her limbs firmly. She tried to struggle from their wicked grips but to no avail. Two energetic young teachers were invited by Mr Pataku. They were given two strong canes to flog Sefakor. They were given the orders to cane her twelve strokes each in turns. They must begin and finish their chore within twenty minutes. Lo and behold, they followed the orders of their master.

Sefakor tried to cope at the beginning but it came to a point when she could no longer stand the pains of the strong lashes landing on the same spot of her tenderly, protruding buttocks. But the youthful teachers who revered Mr Pataku so much   made sure they accomplished the assignment given them within the stipulated time.

Sefakor struggled more than before as the pains grew unbearable. This made it impossible for the strong boys to maintain her in their grips. She stretched her arms and legs hard to free herself and she fell off the table and landed on the ground. The boys quickly pounced on her and pinned her to the ground for the teachers to continue with their freak and vicious persecution. They vented out their spleens on her as if it was a personal vengeance. They removed their shirts and threw the canes at full strength. The canes landed on Sefakor as if they were targeted at a dangerous snake, which had bitten a man to death.   These teachers lost memory of the original number of strokes, therefore, the counting seized abruptly. They were no longer counting the strokes but rather threw the canes haphazardly. They no longer targeted her buttocks as they threw the canes anyhow. The canes landed on every part of the body including her face and breasts. Some strong flogs landed on her waist and tore off strings of beautiful beads around her waist. Most of the beads scattered on the floor. Some of the broken ones penetrated her soft skin and injured her seriously.

At this gruesome moment, Sefakor's body lost control of itself and the unexpected occurred. She urinated into her panties and menstruated at once. This happened when two of the strong canes punched her abdomen. Blood and urine mixed up and soaked her crumpled school uniform. This was the point that some of the girls got fumed and a lady teacher quickly intervened. She pleaded with the headteacher to stop the teachers from what they were doing. In fact, the punishment almost brought humiliation to the entire womanhood.

When they stopped, Sefakor could not get up from the floor due to the severe pains that she suffered. Her younger brother cried all through, right from the time she was invited to climb the table.

After the whipping, Sefakor was dismissed from the school. She was asked to go and look for a school that housed recalcitrant pupils; where there were married couples. The sympathetic brother went to her aid and helped her stand up amidst scornful shouts from fellow pupils. If people laugh at a monkey, they are equally laughing at its carrier. Going by this maxim, some teachers and pupils thought Daada would also deny his sister on that critical moment of hers but that did not happen. He proved to them that blood was really thicker than water.

Daada took his sister to the classroom. They both packed her books and she left the school in shameful pain and disgrace. Surprisingly, Sefakor picked the letter from the ground and put it into her pocket. Probably she wouldn't like anybody else to have access to it. When she was leaving the compound, bellows of "Shame, shame," followed her through the classroom windows till her last step was out of the school compound. The brother advised that they should go home immediately and report the case to their father, Aongo but Sefakor refused to go home. She rather advised Daada to go back to his classroom in order not to suffer any form of unfair treatment like her.

When Sefakor left the school compound, she went and hid in a nearby bush around the school. Owing to the disgrace that she suffered, she became apprehensive of her future in the community. She remained in the bush and never went home till midnight.

Chapter Eight

Aongo did not visit his Limase farm for some days. One day, he told his wife, Afuakuma that some of the palm fruits and bananas might be getting rotten, therefore, they should visit the farm. Aongo would like to inspect his traps and hunt squirrels on the way for a while before reaching the farm. For this reason, he took the lead. Afuakuma would follow after their children who were schooling left for school. Unlike the time of going, on their return journey, they both set off for home together. The journey to farm was smooth for both but the return journey was a bit rough.

On their return, Afuakuma carried their little baby at her back and took the lead. She carried a big bowl of tubers of cassava and cocoyam. She used cassava leaves to cover the root crops and set firewood on top. She held a sturdy cassava stick, which supported her posture under the heavy load. Aongo carried his gun on his left shoulder with a brown farm sack. This farm sack was called *ogudo*. It has a strong string which Aongo hang around the right shoulder. The *ogudo* contained a tuber of yam, a rat and two tree squirrels with some vegetables, which Afuakuma's bowl could not contain. He followed his wife as they both tried to surmount the steep, potholed Limase hill one step after the other.

During this journey, the couple consistently hit their left toes against stones and other obstacles on the pathway. Aongo told Afuakuma that was a sign of bad omen. Something might have been affecting them somewhere. What exactly was the trouble on their way they could not guess right.

At a point, Sefakor's mother experienced a sharp abnormal worry within her womb and complained to the husband. The sign of bad omen, coupled with the abnormal womb disturbances made them profess that something bad might have been occurring to one of their children. Obviously, they did not have answers to these things before they reached home.

Immediately they reached home, they asked of the whereabouts of all their four children. All the children were around except the only girl, Sefakor. None of her siblings including Daada was able to tell about her whereabouts. They all looked for her but could not find her that evening. They then concluded that maybe, she was with one of her friends or was still on the school compound doing something for one of the teachers. Surprisingly, Sefakor did not return home till bedtime.

Actually, Daada thought Sefakor would return home before bedtime that was why he kept quiet over the issue. On the other side of the coin, he did not know how his father would react to the story. Whenever Aongo heard that any of them was punished at school, he would give them the same degree of punishment at home. He always held the philosophy that a teacher was not a mad person to punish a pupil for no wrong done. "A good and obedient child is never punished at school. A punishment to a child at school is a disgrace to the parents at home," Aongo always maintained.

Reporting a punishment from school at home was something Aongo never tolerated. That was why his children never reported at home any punishment meted out to them at school whether fair or unjustified. Perhaps, this was one of the reasons why Daada was reluctant to let the cat out of the bag.

The night was far spent and everybody was about to sleep, yet, Sefakor did not show up. The entire household was becoming jittery. This time round, Daada sensed danger, therefore, he had no better choice than to report the incident to his father and mother. He told them about everything that transpired at school for which Sefakor refused to return home.

The story was in reality a bad one for Afuakuma. She held her belly painfully; she screamed and wept bitterly. She remembered the ordeal she passed through during Sefakor's pregnancy, labour and delivery. She cried and called upon the Ahli shrine and Ovodze goddess to take revenge on her behalf. However, Aongo received the story with a different perception. He aligned the story with his usual philosophy and grew absolutely furious. He became highly annoyed with Sefakor. He said Sefakor would receive another punishment whenever she retuned home. Aongo sat in his old armchair outside his hut, with a belt. He would use the belt to vent his spleen on Sefakor. He would flog her even if she should return at twelve midnight.

Love Me to the End

Corporal Aongo waited for Sefakor till 11:30pm but she did not return. Gradually, Aongo got tired and began dozing off. In conclusion, Aongo vacated his place of duty and went to bed.

Sefakor remained in her hideout for hours. She wept bitterly and cursed her colleagues who held her for the teachers to whip. It was the domesticated mouse who said that he had no problem with the one who caught him, but the one who hit him on the ground. Sefakor had no axe to grind with Messrs Boso and Pataku but vowed not to forgive the teachers who caned her. After all, she committed no crime against them.

Sefakor did not go home for anybody to see her. In the bush where she was hiding, she decided not to remain at Owle again. She would leave the whole area for a town or village, where nobody would either see her or hear about her. Of course, self-pity, self-inferiority and shame wouldn't give her the chance to live at Owle. She envisaged almost everybody in the village would hear about what happened to her.

In the night, around twelve midnight, Sefakor sneaked into the house, smartly picked a few of her vital belongings and left for an unknown destination. It would be a far away place where nobody from Owle including her parents had ever set foot on. Nobody would ever dream and go to that place. The place she headed to was really unknown to herself but only to her maker.

After every five kilometres that she covered, she removed the letter and read it. The words made her happy and gave her more vigour to sail ahead. Sefakor journeyed through many scanty villages, desolate farmhouses and travelled through thick and horrifying forests without rest. She crossed streams, climbed tall mountains and descended into deep valleys for many days but could not find a comfortable place to settle. She became very tired after the fifth day. Owing to tiredness, her speed reduced as she did not stop in any town or village to neither ask for food nor water. In fact, as decided before the set off, she wouldn't like any indigene from Owle to meet her. That was why she decided to cross all towns, villages, forests and bushes tactfully. One day, when her fatigue became too much for her, she sat on a flat stone near an anthill to take a brief rest. Suddenly, she fell into a deep sleep. Before she woke up, it was thirteen minutes past eleven hours in the night.

Sefakor wanted to stay around the anthill for the night before continuing the journey the next day. This decision was dashed when she heard the sound of a host of people approaching. The people seemed to be far away from her, therefore, she hurried to leave the scene before they could get to her. The faster she walked away, the closer the people got to her from behind. In order to avoid them, Sefakor took a bend but they followed suit as if they were trailing her stringently. What baffled her was the speed at which the people were moving. As their voices were so close to her, she decided to take a hurried glance through the trees and see who the people were.

Mysteriously, the noise was just a stone throw from her but she did not see anybody. To be frank, nothing blocked her view from the people's clamour but she did not see any physical being.

Sefakor got a bit scared and could not easily predict the next step of action. Finally, she decided to relax her steps and move at a snail's pace. Suddenly, she was engulfed in a pool of scent of soldier ants. At first, the scent was faint and then it increased and the whole forest area seriously smelt of the ants. It then dawned on her what her grandmother told her about the stench of soldier ants some years back. The grandmother once told her that when you are going to farm and you smell soldier ants, then you must take caution, if not, you will surge into the protectorate of wicked ghosts.

This recollection made Sefakor nervous. All too soon, before she realised, her total body was covered with sizeable goose pimples. It was clear to her that meeting spirits of dead people was imminent. They were just behind her. Nervously, she turned again to find out for the second time who the talkative people were, but she saw nobody again.

In frenzy, Sefakor quickly hid by the narrow path quietly and closed her eyes tightly in order not to see anything dreadful. The noise was now close to her than before and out of curiosity, she opened her eyes to see what was happening around her. Before she realised, there scattered a crowd of strange travellers. Owing to their number, they defiled the bounds of the narrow bush path. All of them were in pure white shrouds – the burial garments; speaking nasally – through their noses. They spoke different languages consecutively. Their language sounded like impoverished Chinese and slipped into simple Nigerian pidgin, then slid into Estuary English of London. It suddenly glided into a rough Liberian Creole and settled on Black English of Black residents of low-income ghettos in the United States of America. Finally, the languages that were conspicuously clear to Sefakor were the Fon of costal and inland Nigeria and coastal Benin and Siya of the people of Avatime in the Volta Region of Ghana and Gen, originally spoken on the coast of Togo. The intonation was undulating; rising and falling of unnatural tune and finally threshed into an incomprehensive oblivion.

Sefakor now saw the travellers clearly with her naked eye. Some of them half naked with various forms of deformities one can think of. Limbless people, people with crushed heads, those who were almost complete skeletons: as frail as AIDS patients of the present generation.

Most of them carried insignificant luggage, which indicated that they were on a journey of no return, hence, they were not so much interested in material things. An intense wind of sorrowful dirges shrouded them. They looked so busy. They were interested in nothing apart from the journey that was ahead of them.

Sefakor identified two people in the crowd. They were a classmate of hers who got drowned in a river and died instantly when they were in class six. The second person was a young lady who passed on with her baby during labour from a nearby village. She was carrying her baby at her back. She bore a disturbing facial semblance, which depicted pain and disappointment.

The people were on an exodus in batches of seven. The last group involved very old but robust women. They were singing traditional dirges with accompanying rattles. One of the songs was so clear to Sefakor.

The market place, the market place.
One day, one day, we shall all meet,
We shall meet those we left behind.
One day, we shall meet in that big market.
Farewell to those alive today;
We are only taking the lead.
We are waiting for you to follow suit.
One by one, you will follow us.

Although the lyrics of the song were very clear, the voices of the singers were naturally very horrifying. The people appeared in different scenes as if they were being projected from a television screen. Firstly, as people who were singing in a convoy and then suddenly changed to corpses laid in state with lots of flowers around them. At a point Sefakor saw only coffins which appeared with a lot of wreaths laid on them. These scenes interchanged one another until the travellers passed by completely.

Sefakor did not hear nor see anything again. Whether the people saw Sefakor or not, she could not tell. She could not tell because none of them acknowledged her presence in any way.

Chapter Nine

Sefakor found it difficult to comprehend the kind of things she experienced so far. She saw a great difference between human life in a town and things that happen at night in thick isolated forests when human beings fall asleep and rest in their comfortable beds. "You cannot believe some of these things when you are told unless you see things for yourself," Sefakor contemplated.

There was a flip of flash back. This time it dawned on Sefakor clearly that she met with people from a different world: the world of dead people. Sefakor trembled convulsively and got frozen to her bones. She saw clearly that she was wadding in the valley of death. She met the dark side of life with its haunts and nastiness. At that moment, Sefakor was shoved into a world of great uncertainty. Going back home was unthinkable. Moving ahead was highly perilous and remaining in that forest was too suicidal for her survival. She was totally confused and did not exactly know the next step to take.

The scenario she experienced was that a host of ghosts went to market and were on their way home in a convoy. They were on a return journey to their place of abode, which was a nearby cemetery. That was the time Sefakor met them.

When things became clear to Sefakor, she removed a special ointment made from frankincense from her polythene bag and smeared her toes, fingers, temple, nape and her hair and smeared some on her face. This ointment was given to her by her deceased grandmother. She gave it to Sefakor before she died. The day she was going to farm with her grandmother and they encountered ghosts that was what they used to prevent the ghosts from harming them.

Sefakor was lucky she took this ointment along with her when she was embarking on her journey. The smell of this body mist could drive away witches and other evil spirits. This was a strong weapon she had with her throughout the journey.

Immediately after anointing her volatile parts, every spiritual activity ceased and she regained her total consciousness. After a spell of time, Sefakor took her polythene bag and continued her precarious voyage.

After walking for a few metres, she reached a place where she started locating old graves and suddenly bumped into recent ones. It was a big cemetery that she got into. This cemetery was desolate and absolutely quiet. It was located between two towns. It was rumoured that ghosts from the area used to haunt people occasionally in these two towns. That was the reason why the cemetery was sited far away from the two towns that used to bury dead people there. The cemetery was clear, yet the thick foliage of huge trees around held a vague terror over the whole place; making the cemetery a horrible site, especially, at night.

Though there was no hurricane lantern or gaslight at this forest cemetery, the place was miraculously well-lit.

Sefakor tried to trace the source of light but that was undoubtedly unworkable.

For her safety, Sefakor sat on one of the hidden gravestones to rest, in order that no hidden person would see her from any corner. Then there emerged a cold whirlwind which engrossed the tree tops; flapping the branches in a thrilling manner. Within the twinkling of an eye, the excited branches unveiled powerful flying lanterns with very bright, sharp, white colour. These lanterns were more powerful than one hundred watts electric bulbs. They flew from one angle of the cemetery to another. They crisscrossed one another in a fascinating mode. Finally, two flying coffins were uncovered. They were shrouded by a bliss of flood lights.

It was a coven of witches and wizards that was going to the cemetery that night. They were going to bury two people who were then alive when everybody was deep asleep. Though the people were alive, these witches had finished eating their flesh already in spirit and they were burying them. This was a terrific scene to watch. Witches displayed their sharp, long teeth with powerful, jagged swords. Sefakor crept quietly and hid under a small patch of bush on the outskirt of the cemetery. This was where she remained till daybreak.

The next day, Sefakor fell seriously sick and could not leave the bush where she was hiding near the cemetery. She spent almost the whole day there.

In the afternoon, around 1.00pm an alarm was raised. It was obvious that there was danger. The alarm raged loud and louder and engulfed the whole environment including the cemetery area. A prominent man resident in Kumasi, who visited his parents in one of the two towns died immediately he reached his destination. The news of his death was sent home that hot afternoon through telegram message. Sefakor then told herself that they had finished with the first one.

In the evening, the other town was thrown into a state of sorrow when another disaster struck. A promising secondary school girl on vacation met her untimely death under a disheartened circumstance. This girl was returning from farm with her mother and siblings that late afternoon and a snake fell from a tree and bit her. All efforts made to save her from the poison of the venomous snake failed and she passed on before sun set. Of course, the death of the two important indigenes in the physical realm was imminent once that task was already accomplished in the spiritual realm by witches and wizards.

A cold wind blew through the branches of trees in the vicinity. Dogs barked and rumbled along ceaselessly. People cried and wailed over the demises but then, the die was cast and no amount of witchery or prayers could prevent the crossing of the Rubicon.

Sefakor wished she had some one beside her to narrate some of her bitter experiences to, but that was impracticable. It was at this critical juncture that it dawned on Sefakor that her encounter with the ghosts was an indication that they were aware of receiving visitors. That was the reason why they went to market on that night for shopping. It was a sign of Ghanaian hospitality even among the immortal beings. In fact, this sequence of events made Sefakor become frightened and decided not to spend a minute in that area again.

Truly, Sefakor could not live in the forest near the cemetery the next day. This was due to fear and trembling over what she experienced in the night and what followed during the day. She carried her small luggage and continued the journey to her unknown destination without hesitation.

Chapter Ten

The journey ahead of Sefakor seemed to be more terrifying than the previous one.

Sefakor now seemed to galley through the valley of death. The voyage was full of miserable daydreams. She decoded cries of wild animals; she shook hands with monsters and met with powerful spiritual beings face to face.

At a point Sefakor became fed up with the state of affairs. She felt the disgrace and humiliation she would have suffered at Owle would have been less irritating than what she was going through. She then decided to go back home to beg her parents and teachers to forgive her and accept her back as a prodigal daughter and student.

Sefakor's mind was shot into a state of uncompromising nostalgia. She looked back at home and fond memories resurrected from their dungeons. She remembered how she used to play with her siblings and schoolmates during moonlit nights. She remembered some of their play songs and intoned one popular one. Then she flipped to another page. She recollected the days of sports and games when pupils of all basic schools from Bagome, Owle and Obane used to meet and play games: football for boys, netball for girls and volleyball for both. She flashed back the interschool cultural festivals. And now the story time after evening meals was hoisted in her upset mind like a national flag. Quickly, the Friday evening C.Y.B and C.Y.O meetings flashed her mind vividly. And then *borborbor* nights before the rice festival dominated her mind and flew off. She felt homesick and remembered her mother and siblings dearly. All got sufficient food to eat and she was reduced to nothing but a level below that of a domestic animal. She had no alternative than to feed on cassava leaves. If foreign land is not good for you, you must trace your hometown. She settled on going back to Owle her home village. She was confident her parents and friends would accord her a rousing welcome back home.

Sefakor did not take a straight route and her path was a winding one, therefore, going back home was unfeasible. Taking a critical look at the web in which she entangled herself, she decided to move ahead until she got a final place to settle.

 Sefakor journeyed on and walked for miles for days. One day, Sefakor sat under a mango tree to rest and eat some ripe mangoes, which were on the ground. This tree was in a very thick forest, which seemed inaccessible to many human beings. She relaxed under this tree and started gobbling the mangoes. Suddenly, she heard a cry, which resembled that of a baby. Sefakor got startled as she did not envisage the presence of any human being in that bleak forest.

Out of the blue, a baby fell from the top of the tree with its umbilical cord hanging around its navel. The baby landed right in front of her. The little baby cried very loud, as if it was just brought forth by someone on top of the mango tree. She was scared as there was no sign of human habitation miles around the area. She sensed danger. She felt it could be a spirit that turned into a baby. Sefakor quickly stood up, picked her things and hurriedly left the place. The baby cried the loudest when it saw that Sefakor was leaving it behind. This touched her feminine heart. She therefore decided to return to the baby to at least keep it company for a while. Before she could reach where the baby was, another one fell with the same condition and a third one right on one of her shoulders. Within the twinkling of an eye, these three babies fell from the tree like ripe papaws falling from a tired pawpaw tree. They all lay naked in front of her and looked directly into her eyes with stern, prime faces.

Miraculously, the first baby grew fast and became older than the rest. The second one like magic developed faster than the first and quickly developed speech. This baby started communicating with Sefakor but she spoke a strange language which Sefakor could not decipher.

Sefakor was startled and got dazed by the turn of events. Soon, she started picking few of the words from the cherub-like baby's lingo. Gradually, mutual intelligibility developed and both Sefakor and the cherub understood each other's languages. The baby asked Sefakor what had brought her to that forbidden forest. Sefakor courageously narrated her freak story to the baby. The baby told Sefakor that they were the servants of the forest. They travelled from some dreadful forests in Africa and came to settle in that virgin forest for a while. It mentioned the names of their dwelling forests in Africa; noticeably, the revered evil forests of Nigeria. According to the baby, they were among twins discarded and dumped in some evil forests in the olden days. Now, they developed into small cherubs, which assist people who got stranded in thick forests in Africa and elsewhere. They travelled at the speed of lighting to whichever place their assistance was required. This made it possible for them to assist a good number of deprived people like Sefakor.

The baby told Sefakor a lot of things. "We were informed of your plight and were sent to rescue you while on duty in a forest in Pretoria in South Africa," she concluded her dialogue with Sefakor.

After the talk, the baby led Sefakor and showed her where to pass before she could survive the rest of her journey. Otherwise, the time of her doom was at hand. The other babies who changed into fully grown teenagers burst into singing of melodic traditional love songs and progressively, all of them flew away as powerful wingless birds.

Chapter Eleven

Sefakor's journey had lasted for seven months. She had not yet come to a place of abode, therefore the journey must continue. She walked for another full day and became more exhausted than ever. Walking about seven kilometers away from where she met the babies, the day turned into dusk. Sefakor could no longer see properly. She, therefore, decided to pass the night at that place. At that crucial moment, she saw a shady tree with thick foliage few metres ahead of her. Sefakor targeted the tree and paced towards it. When she reached there, she saw that it was a good place for her to pass the night. She put the polythene bag, which contained her belongings down and spread her cloth on the ground and lay on it. She used one of the sizeable stones around as a pillow. Shortly, a cold tender wind blew and sent her into a deep slumber. Sefakor slept soundly throughout the night. In fact, she did not have the chance to sleep like that for several months.

The tree under which Sefakor slept was a meeting place for a collection of birds. The birds often did eat and play on top of that tree. That dawn, the birds came to their entertainment and refreshment ground again. Of course, the early bird catches the early worm. They were there in their numbers that morning to peck the fruits and wait for the morning to arrive.

The birds got busy and buried into their mission. By chance, one of the birds suddenly caught a glimpse of Sefakor sleeping under the tree. It got frightened and yelped. It raised an alarm that caught the attention of the rest of the birds on that tree and those on nearby trees. Quickly, they all gathered at a spot on top of the tree under which the fearful creature was pictured. Now, other birds from the surrounding trees which got wind of what was happening sent their delegates to join the team. They all cried in unison in order to expose what had invaded their territory that early morning. These birds chirped with different tunes and different voices. The blend of the voices of these birds sounded like beautiful music in ears that heard it from afar.

A hunter went hunting in the night and could not find any animal to kill. The cries of these birds attracted the attention of the hunter. Basically, he went out hunting to look for a rodent for a good meal for a visitor he received the previous day. He combed the entire forest but could not locate any game for the calibre of his gun to gobble up.

When he heard the loud cries of the birds, he concluded that it was a big snake that they were hooting at. Otherwise, it could be a wild animal that they were scaring out of their haven. It became a good chance for the disappointed hunter to try his luck. Obviously that was his last chance. He gauged the tree and traced it meticulously. When he got closer to the tree, he saw that a big animal was sleeping under it. He perceived it as the type that his gun could conquer. He tiptoed gently with his toes firm on the ground. He got the distance at which he could fire without missing the target. He settled and hoisted his hunting light on his forehead properly. He saw the animal more clearly. Unfortunately, he was standing in an army of driver ants. He wanted to shoot but could not contain the sting of the ants and so he lost control of the gun and the weapon fell with a clunk. This could wake the animal up but this animal made no attempt to escape the wrath of the hunter.

He presumed it was deeply asleep as a result of tiredness or else, it was the lazy type. Now he set the nozzle directly on the mammal. He located the trigger of the gun and set his index finger on it firmly.

"One, two, three, shoot!" His brain commanded him to act, but there was a missing link between the finger and the brain, hence a relaxation. The hand failed to respond to the command. It seemed to him that he was still far away from the animal, therefore, he decided to draw closer than before. He drew closer again; set himself for the shootout. He made all attempts to make sure that the animal would not get a wind of him and run away. He set the gun straight on the animal and wanted to shoot. Then the cries of the birds suddenly increased to an abnormal level, as if they were shouting at him; warning him to desist from what he was about to do.

This confused him and made him lower his hungry weapon impulsively. He took a breath; a deep breath of course, and stretched his neck to take another critical look at the game. Coincidentally, the animal flashed its arm in the air and put it back quietly. He saw clearly that the hand resembled that of a monkey.

"When have monkeys resolved to descend and sleep on the ground like this?" he soliloquized silently. This state of affairs baffled the hunter because he knew that as for monkeys, they sleep on top on trees: never on the floor like that.

The hunter did not lose his grips yet. He gathered all courage and got nearer to the animal in question. To his utter surprise, there slept a young beautiful teenage girl; deeply asleep. Her clothes were drenched in dawn dews. The hunter became highly astonished and wanted to scream out of shock but that was inappropriate for a famous hunter like him. He was the type that could be counted on during war with a neighbouring village.

Totally dumbfounded, Liwabi sat quietly near the girl. This was the first time he had had such an experience throughout his forty years of hunting. He looked at the girl again and again. He raised his face and turned to the east and thanked the gods that they did not permit him to kill the young woman. That would have been too much for him to bear. You have no justification of murdering a man who has not provoked you. Liwabi knew about this from his childhood when he used to follow his late father, Bobofo on hunting expeditions. That was why the hunters had principles which they followed. One of these conventions was: "Don't fire when you cannot see the animal clearly." He vowed never to shed innocent blood and that never happened to him yet. He also thanked the birds for what they did to stop him from killing such an innocent, pretty, young beauty. Looking at the level of Sefakor's beauty Liwabi concluded that the maiden was not a human being but a goddess.

Sefakor now got to know about the presence of a human being. She woke up from her sleep partially and raised her head and saw the hunter. She showed no sign of agitation but rather retired into another round of sleep.

On account of the fact that the hunter saw Sefakor as a goddess, he did not ask her any question. The hunter did not make any attempt to look for any game again. He took his hungry gun, empty sack, machete and left for home.

When Liwabi reached home, he narrated his ordeal to the chief hunter and fetish priest, Avese. Through Avese, all experienced hunters and medicine men in the village got to know about Liwabi's encounter. All and sundry settled on the fact that it was a deity that wanted to stay with Liwabi. "He is a lucky man," they reaffirmed. Ataalu, one of the experienced hunters narrated a similar story about an old hunter who became fabulously rich overnight through such an encounter. All of them advised Liwabi to do what that old hunter did when he met the deity in a forest at dawn.

Liwabi was advised to let his wife prepare a nice meal that morning and send it under the tree where the goddess was sleeping. He should also add a big pot of water and a calabash to the food. He should continue doing that until the goddess departed from the place. From the word go, he would say goodbye to poverty all things being equal. Wonders and mercies from benevolent gods would follow him abundantly. Poverty would be very far away from him and his family, even the generation yet unborn.

Liwabi accepted this counsel without a bit of challenge. That morning, Liwabi slaughtered one of his fat goats and his wife pounded fufu. The woman served the food, fetched water and added a calabash to it. By noonday, Liwabi and one of his sons took the items to the bush and placed them at a place where Sefakor could see them.

Before Sefakor woke from a nap, real food and water were ready. Sefakor saw genuine food made of pepper and salt for months. She dashed to where the food was without a speck of question about the source of it. She ate all the food, licked her fingers thoroughly and drank a calabash full of water. Later, she used the rest of the water to have her bath.

From that day Sefakor never lacked food and water. Like manna from heaven, food and water were regular every morning, every evening. This made it possible for Sefakor to take that place as a safe temporary place of abode for years.

After few days, Liwabi built a small hut under the big tree for Sefakor and equipped it with a mat, pillow, a big cloth and other vital items, which Sefakor could use. Sefakor made the place nice and dwelled in that forest. For years, rain and sunshine never disturbed her.

Sefakor never met Liwabi face to face. She made sure she avoided him. Sefakor knew the exact time

Liwabi used to bring her food and water. She always made it a point to leave the hut and hide somewhere before Liwabi arrived. She would then go back immediately Liwabi had left. As if it was an agreement between the two of them, Liwabi also made sure he never spent time under that tree. Therefore, throughout the period Sefakor lived in the little hut, under the big tree, in the isolated forest, he never met her again.

Often, the birds used to visit the tree to eat, sing and play. These activities of the birds were a good source of entertainment for Sefakor. One evening, the birds came to sing one of their melodious songs. The lyrics in the song were clearer than those of the previous songs produced by the same birds. It appeared as if some human beings were singing along side the birds. The song was one of the songs children of Owle used to sing during moonlit nights when Sefakor was at home. This song was not only associated with children, but also adults as well. Adults used to sing it during *treza* ceremonies.

Treza was a night they used to celebrate for bachelors and spinsters. Two, two, God created us; therefore, no one has the justification for being a bachelor or spinster. In this respect, the people of Owle used to organise the *treza* ceremony for those who were mature but could not find their partners yet, for one reason or the other.

The night was purposely meant for them to try their luck once again. The night was always full of love stories and love songs to make love a thirst and an appealing craze to those who did not value it. Living alone does not grow a village into a town. It would rather diminish a big town to a small hamlet. If this behaviour was not nipped in the bud, then after some years, it will be only the fencing poles that could narrate the history that human beings had once lived in that part of the country. This is a strong belief of the elderly people of Owle. This made them institute the treza for young ladies and gentlemen.

Sefakor bore all remembrance of things which usually went on during the treza night. It used to be a night that both married and unmarried men of Owle cherished – night of perfume and banquet fragrance. One of the big borborbor drums used to boom: " *Omono omonoe, xe wota mor tse wota nu, xe wota nu tse wota mor!*" It would quickly translate the beat into pidgin: "*Today be today, you no go see, you go hear, you no go hear, you go see!*" This drum beat used to receive a round of applause village-wide. It used to draw people to the place in no time. This was the song the birds sang that night.

I love you with all my heart.
You too do same to me.
That you will be mine for ever.
You will be mine for ever;
Till the end of age.

Sefakor sang the song with the birds. This made her exceedingly homesick. She remembered the day Abrokwa invited her to dance with him. Abrokwa's picture now covered the face of her mind. She pulled out

Abrokwa's letter, and read it over and over again until she fell into a benevolent sound sleep.

Chapter Twelve

After Sefakor had left home, her teachers, parents, classmates and friends felt she would return in no time. This was what most of the recalcitrant children of Owle used to do to threaten those who punish them. They would leave the village and after a day or two, they would resurface. They have nowhere to go after all. The people were there in anticipation that should Sefakor keep long at her hideout at all, it would just be three or four days. She could, however, remain at her hideout for a week or two if she should meet a Good Samaritan on her way.

"She will definitely come back home as a prodigal daughter," her father used to tell the mother.

The father planned that if she returned, she would never receive that kind of reception accorded the prodigal son in the Bible. They won't make that mistake. She would receive the toughest punishment that a disciplined father could give to a notorious daughter. This would deter her younger siblings and peers from that kind of unacceptable and irresponsible behaviour.

Sefakor's parents' mind clung on and brooded over the kind of punishment to give to her if she returned. For two fortnights Sefakor did not show up. After this period, panic and anxiety of seeing their daughter set in.

Although the chief of the village knew of Sefakor's disappearance, he did not make any attempt for his *tsorfo* group to look for her. He expected her relatives to raise the alarm before the whole village would join. He expected the family to report the case to him and his subjects at least with a pot of palm-wine according to the custom. Nobody did that so the chief held his peace. "If you raise the pot, others would assist you to catch the mouse under it," the chief told one of his elders.

The disappearance of Sefakor and the behaviour of the family were so stinking but many indigenes of Owle had no alternative than to fasten their gobs.

Two months went down the era without anybody from the west, east, north or south reporting of seeing Sefakor anywhere. This was the moment when close relatives' emotions got stirred up to the seriousness of the case. Eyes began developing the red colour. The family then saw that it was expedient to report the incident to the chief. One early morning, they sent a pot of palm-wine to the chief and told him that one of their daughters by name Sefakor Abla Atipo was missing for such a period. After going into the case, the chief fined Sefakor's parents two rams and four pots of palm-wine. He ordered them to present the items in full before the village would be informed about the incident. They begged and the items were reduced by half to enable them present the items immediately as time was running out. This they did in no time. The same day the chief summoned his subjects for thorough deliberation on the issue. Most of them suggested that the teachers in the centre of the matter should be invited for their side of the story to be taken. Before then, there was a rumour in the village suggesting that the headteacher who pronounced and supervised Sefakor's punishment got himself into a serious trouble and had left Owle. He impregnated the girls' prefect of the school and education officers were hunting for him. Owing to this, he left Owle for fear of being arrested and dismissed from his post. Despite this rumour, the chief invited the teachers involved in the case and gave them a week to look for the girl, else they would face the full rigours of the laws of the land.

Later, the chief and his Council of Elders ordered Sefakor's family to send delegations to their family members living in Kumasi, Kpalime in Togo, Port Novo in Benin and Badagri in Nigeria to ask whether Sefakor was with them. The family followed this order without hesitation. In fact, none of these kinsmen responded in the affirmative. The chief followed all events leading to discovery of Sefakor with all diligence. He thought seriously about the episode and concluded that Sefakor disappeared for a long time, therefore, if she died somewhere, by that time, the body would have decomposed completely hence, a forest search would be a vain expedition.

Sefakor's parents had lost all hope, as there seemed to be no sign of Sefakor's return nor survival. Her mother lamented day in and day out and was reduced to the size of a broom stick overnight. She starved herself for several days. She thought that would bring back her daughter but all to no avail. She said, she wouldn't eat until she met her daughter face to face – either dead or alive. Sefakor's mother pinned the disaster that bedeviled her home on Abrokwa and his friend Apati. She wanted Abrokwa and his parents to bring her loving daughter back to her by hook or by crook. Whether Abrokwa and his parents could bring Sefakor back home was a tight spot.

Chapter Thirteen

One evening, there was chaos on Abrokwa's parents' compound. Sefakor's father, Aongo returned from farm and saw Sefakor's school uniform displayed on a dry line. He got enraged by the sight of the uniform and took his gun. He rushed to Abrokwa's house to finish him and his parents off. It took the intervention of some powerful juju men to over power him. They cast series of spells on him that enabled them collect the gun from him. Else, it would have been a nasty scene for the village on that day.

One Friday morning the chief let the drummer sound the emergency talking drums to summon the whole village of Owle. All and sundry trooped to *lineneme*: the market place, where the whole village used to converge. There the chief officially announced the disappearance of Sefakor to the whole village.

Zando, one of the women in the village reported that on the said day, she returned from farm lately. Before taking the last lap to the village, she met a girl with a small luggage made of a woman's waist cloth and with a small polythene bag on hand. The girl bypassed her at an extraordinary speed and descended the Limase hill at full speed as it was fast   getting dark. The girl was crying profusely as if she was a ghost hastening home to the ancestors. According to Zando, in one of the girl's hands was a small bottle that resembled that of DDT insecticide. So, if Sefakor was the girl she met and did not return for all these days, then there was no doubt that she committed suicide and she might have perished somewhere.

Apam Okoto, a hunter also said he met her on the same day, around 8:00 pm wading her way through bushes at the foot of Ogborhu mountain. Later, he saw a wild leopard and shot at it but the bullets couldn't penetrate its pelt. He did not gauge it properly and so, it did not die but ran away from him. It was a hungry, powerful, sturdy leopard. It was barely wounded, therefore became wilder. After a spell of time, it seemed to him the leopard had an encounter with the girl in the forest. He clearly heard the screams of a human being far away but after a spell, everything ceased. "Oh, the leopard might have devoured this innocent girl," he told the people with his two arms raised across his head.

These and other revelations sent fears and anxiety down the spines of the inhabitants of Owle. It was now becoming obvious that Sefakor should no longer be considered among those on the land of the living. Many people put out conflicting rumours regarding Sefakor's disappearance. Some of these rumours were unfounded and contradictory. They were without an iota of proof and they held no water. Those that seamed to suggest the truth were rather rumours of horrible nightmares. One of Sefakor's friends also narrated her nightmare to people. She mentioned that one day, she was going to toilet on the outskirts of the village at sundown when she suddenly bumped into Sefakor. According to her, Sefakor was in a pure white cloak with two wreaths in hand; hurrying towards the direction of the main cemetery. Before she could raise an alarm, Sefakor vanished completely.

The string of stories about Sefakor ate into time. Finally, the chief decided that whether Sefakor drank poison and died or her mortal body was shredded by a carnivorous animal, her bones at least could be found somewhere in the forest.

The chief referred to his archives of experience and ordered his men to move towards the four directions of the village in search of Sefakor. Seeing her alive was distant from reality as of that time. Sefakor resurfacing alive on Owle land could only come out of fantasy. Her decomposed mortal remains were what exactly the men were gravely trailing. The chief again sent a word to the people of the surrounding towns and villages for their men to assist in the search.

The search parties combed all the forests that surrounded the Orgborhu mountain and beyond for days. But there was no sign of even a wrecked casket of a dead monkey. They therefore returned home without any story about where exactly Sefakor gave up her ghost.

One dawn, Sefakor's grand mother, Kalai woke up from a strange dream. In the dream, her granddaughter, Sefakor was laid in state in a virgin forest. She, Kalai, was the only human being around the corpse among wild beasts. She was keeping vigil overnight; preventing the wild animals from carrying the decorated body away. It was a very tough time for her in the dream as some of these animals snarled and waggled their tails terribly. They were pushing in with all force to carry the body away by all means. These animals claimed the beautifully adorned body belonged to their king.

Kalai woke up that dawn bathed in sweat – panting. She raised an alarm on top of her voice. The alarm attracted all manner of people in the vicinity. They all dashed into her small thatched hut to ascertain what the trouble was. In fact, what Kalai saw in her dream confirmed the rumour that Sefakor was devoured by an untamed animal.

Kalai narrated the dream to the people and reassured them that Sefakor was dead and gone.

"She was killed by wild animals in a thick forest." She turned to the family members and told them this.

Kalai was an old woman both young and old revered in the village. She was once a fetish priestess whose visions hardly missed the mark. Those were the days before she was baptised into the Catholic Church. People therefore still held that trust in her, therefore, her vision vilified all possibilities of Sefakor's survival.

This latest development made all women burst into singing dirges that dawn. Kalai led the trail through the snaky alleys of the village. This was what they used to do whenever an indigene lost his or her life under a mysterious circumstance.

They sang this dirge mournfully, while crying and wailing without rest:

Where a tortoise dies,
He leaves his property there.
He rests quietly in his coffin.
No-one to bury tortoise in life;
No mourner to bury tortoise,
That's why tortoise buries himself.
Tortoise buries himself in life.

They continued doing this until the bright morning sun rose from its slumber before they dispersed.

Chapter Fourteen

The entire village of Owle now got it clear that Sefakor's journey on earth ended prematurely. But one pertinent issue still lingered on. Even if an indigene of Owle died in the middle of the sea, the corpse must be brought home for burial. If not the entire body, then at least some of her pubic hairs and finger nails must be brought home for interment. This custom would transmit the dead person's spirit to the ancestral world. Without this, the deceased person's spirit would never rest. It would remain in the village to haunt people until the right thing is done.

Both young and old at Owle assumed that by all means, Sefakor's spirit would not rest. And her ghost would punish the village with a severe plague if her body was not brought home and buried in line with the traditions of Owle. If her spirit should remain in the forest for a year, there would be a disaster in the whole village. The elderly people remembered what happened to their neighbours of Kukrum, some thirty years back. A young man committed suicide in the bush and the body was not traced and brought home for burial. The gods got angry and killed all the chiefs and most of their subjects within a month for what they regarded as irresponsible behaviour. The gods did not understand why the chiefs should forget about the oath of allegiance they swore to the people they governed.

The chief of Owle commanded his *tsorfo* men to go deep into all the major forests around Owle. He cautioned them not to return home unless they got Sefakor's body – dead or alive. They obliged and promised the chief that they would do exactly what he expected from them. As warriors, they made themselves ready physically and spiritually within the twinkling of an eye. They sang a lot of war songs to re-energize themselves before setting off. They divided themselves into four factions. Each party faced one of the cardinal points of the village – east, west, north and south. They all traversed deep into their side of the forest that confronted them. They went deep into the forests as the chief directed, leaving no stone unturned. They roamed the forests from one corner to the other. They searched from the treetops down to small holes. They went the extra mile by rolling all suspicious large stones and rocks that had holes under them. They broke into caves of wild animals. They traced all tracks of wild animals and hunters but all to no avail. They travailed all day to even far dangerous parts of the forests, but they could not gather even the clay of a dead mouse. They feared going back home to report the vain expedition to the chief and the entire village.

Meanwhile, no indigene of the village went to farm on that day. They all waited anxiously for the return of the brave men who they trusted could bring home Sefakor's body. A spirit of black bile held delicate terror over the entire village. Of course, the people were of all hope that with Zibo and Piaho among the group members the men would certainly bring home the mortal remains of the young lady, Sefakor. Zibo and Piaho had special powers from Dahome. They could command the spirit of a dead person to speak to them. Therefore, the people trusted that the duo could command Sefakor's ghost to direct them to where exactly her remains were.

Lines in the human palm started disappearing. It was therefore obvious that men could no longer see clearly. They had no alternative than to withdraw from the forests. The search at that moment seemed to be a futile one. All the four parties began to signal one another. The message was that the day was over and night was at hand. Wild animals could pose problems to them if they should remain in the dreaded forests till dusk. They communicated through whistling, loud cries and yells so that even those who were far in the forest valleys could hear. In a short time, the message went through and all parties decided to converge at the foot of Gayi mountain. That was the place they were to gather and discuss what message to send home to the anxious chief and citizens. After all, they wouldn't like to be branded as cowards. They needed tangible reasons which at least could assuage the apprehension of the people. After that they would go back home quietly. After all, there was no way they could remain in the forest because of a vain search.

All the leaders called on all their men to follow the order to meet the other members at one spot. They stopped .the search and waded towards the mountain but still with curious eyes.

Chapter Fifteen

The people at home were now tired of waiting. Talkative people and rumour mongers took over the day. They fabricated and disseminated all sort of stories. The period was naturally ripe for all ears to pay attention and believe anything that was said about Sefakor at that crucial moment. This gave the opportunity to all kinds of tall tales to crisscross almost all ears of the village.

At exactly ten minutes past six, an alarm was raised somewhere in the forest. This alarm was coming from Piaho. A point in time, for a short period though, Piaho separated himself from other members of his group. This was when it became lucid that they would go home without a message of hope.

By the alarm, members of Piaho's group jostled to the forest involuntarily to get to the spring of the terrible cry. Members of other groups also heard the alarm. They doubled up and dashed to that side of the forest to join their comrades. When they all reached the spot, they saw a tattered piece of cloth belonging to a human being. Few steps beyond that were dry bones of a skull and limbs of an adolescent person.

Fear gripped the men as what the saw depicted the skeleton of Sefakor whom they were searching for. In fact, it was Piaho, the man of shocking bravery who discovered the skeleton. He vowed that they would never return home without any information about Sefakor. At that point it was obvious that they located Sefakor's dead body.

Some rituals were supposed to be performed before somebody could touch the remains. Piaho was ready for that. He removed a bottle of local liquor; *akpeteshie* from his old haversack. He poured a glass full, held it in his left hand, removed his *tokota* sandals, faced the west and poured libation:

Agoo, agoo, agooo!
Almighty Agyepor,
We call you.
Ovude, Reidi, Kalatabui, Bente shrines,
We invite you.
Torgbe Okatsie, Kotoko, Ogbogi and all ancestors,
We invite you.
Mama Danzo, Onetsi, Golo, Apataku
Take your drink!
Today, we invite all of you, not on a happy note,
Our daughter Sefakor has left the world prematurely,
We thank you for leading us to her remains.
We are conveying her body and soul home for burial,
You were with us from the beginning to this time
Guide us to reach home safely with her.
Great Agyepor, you sneezed and fishes died in rivers.
You defecated, and mountains came into being.
You passed water, and great rivers were formed.
Ogidigidi! As the sun sets today,
It should set with this kind of evil tidings.

We expect good news, but not news of blood death.
Let Sefakor's spirit rest with you and ancestors.
Our gods and ancestors,
Take your drink.
Those who don't drink in public
Take yours from there. (*He poured the rest at a different place*)

They all raised alarms right after the prayer and the courageous ones gathered the substances and wrapped them in broad plantain leaves, which they tied on a bamboo pole for two men to carry. Amidst masculine cries, which were masked up in alarms and war songs, all the men marched home with brisk, simultaneous gallops.

Traditionally, whenever a thing of that nature happened at Owle, all the animals which were part of the felony must be brought home. When a snake bites any indigene to death or a wild animal killed somebody, all animals considered to partake in the conspiracy must be brought home. They would be hooted at, at the centre of the village and set ablaze in a bonfire. Animals which normally suffered from this fate were snails, scorpions, snakes, mice, and lizards.

From the time the men got to the bones, they immediately started hunting for these animals. By tradition, the body must not reach home without them. That would signify that these wicked animals have won the battle over human beings. Some people challenged the inclusion of snails on the list of these animals. But elders usually said that sometimes the other animals did use snails as bates to lure human beings into their tracks. Also, snails did lick the blood of the victims on the ground so that humans cannot trace the source of the unpleasant incident.

By 9.00 pm, the men reached home with the remains. People's minds were already primed that Sefakor died in the bush long time ago. Therefore, they were not surprised when Piaho and his men brought home the remains that night.

The chief and his elders were invited to examine the remains after which the entire village would be summoned. After meticulous examination, they all agreed that was the decomposed body of Sefakor. However, there was one skeptic among the old men. This man was called Agude.

Customs of Owle demanded that such a corpse must be buried immediately it reached home so that such a thing would not happen again. Thus, the cold windy mourning weather did not stop the people from burying the body that night. Talking drums roared and roared again and again and all inhabitants trouped to the centre of Owle. That was where the death of Sefakor was announced to the people officially.

That kind of death was *kuwletse*, which is tragic death in an accident, therefore, the corpse was not allowed into the village by custom. She either committed suicide or was killed by a wild animal. Either of the two would be classified as blood death. Therefore, her remains were left on the outskirts of the village under a small shed erected that night with palm branches. That was where they laid the undignified mortal remains of Sefakor; cloaked in plantain leaves.

Powerful men and some relatives went there in the early part of the night to pay their last respect. The bones were then wrapped in a white calico fabric provided by Sefakor's family. That was where various rites were performed and finally the body was carried by few young men and was sent to the final resting place of accident victims. Paled, scattered dirges from old women trailed the remains till they were dropped into a narrow grave. Some of Sefakor's belongings that she left behind were added to the   bones and buried that night.

Aongo followed the people steadily with his short, single-barrel gun speechlessly. He tied a big red band around his head. He was conspicuously seen as the chief mourner and there was no doubt about that. Immediately Sefakor's body was lowered into the grave, Aongo approached the burial chamber and fired three shots inside it. He fired other three shots into the sky and left the cemetery for home in tears. That was the first time people saw tears in Aongo's eyes. Aongo was described as someone who ate tortoise's head because tears never dripped from his eyes from childhood but that night broke the norm.

Afuakuma, Sefakor's mother was hard to console. She followed the remains of her loving daughter closely, despite efforts made by her friends and close relatives to prevent her from going to the graveside. She cried miserably as she stood there until the grave was completely concealed with earth.

Love Me to the End

The following day, Sefakor's classmates went to her graveside with a cross with this lettering: "Love me to the end; don't leave me on the way."

They erected the cross at the head of the grave. The words were boldly written that many people could see and read. Yes, these were the words Sefakor wrote under Abrokwa's letter when she finished reading it. The classmates did that to indicate that Sefakor died as a result of love.

After the burial, a time was set for her funeral to send her home properly to the ancestors. It was just a one week interval.

There was a vigil on Friday, where the young ones in the village showed their last respect to Sefakor and mourned her for the last. The following morning the funeral itself began. Many people with family ties from nearby towns and villages attended the funeral. They were there to show their solidarity with Sefakor's clansmen. The funeral attracted many young men and women because Sefakor was a famous sports girl and was known by many in the surrounding towns and villages.

After six, the funeral ended and anything about Sefakor became history from that day.

Chapter Sixteen

Agude drank palm-wine and became intoxicated. He sang a funny *gabada* song:

They call you Elizabeth,
You are called Mary,
But you don't go to church.
The church bell rings
The pastor is preaching
But you are not in church.

He invited his wife who was then peeling cassava to draw herself closer to him. Ayasa was reluctant but she decided to join him.

"Agude, why do you men always associate everything that is unpalatable to women?" his wife asked him jokingly.

"Why that question? What is your problem?" Agude asked his wife furiously.

"Agude, I thought you would use names like Emmanuel and Abraham in your song instead of Paulina and Felicia! "

"Am I the one who composed the song? Ayasa, be careful!" Agude warned his wife.

The wife however told him that she was just joking.

Love Me to the End

"But it is high time you men stopped behaving that way!" Ayasa added.

The exchange subsided and Agude introduced a new topic. Perhaps that was the reason why he invited his wife.

"Ayasa, something has been bothering my mind and I would like to purge it this evening," he began. Agude pulled a basket of maize and began to shell as his wife was also peeling cassava and at the same time paying attention to him.

"Aya, the people of Owle are funny. The chief and his elders are mere comedians. Piaho and Zibo gathered bones of a chimpanzee and deceived the whole village that they were the remains of a teenage girl. And Aongo of all people: an old soldier, who went to peacekeeping at Burma, Congo, Abyssinia, Lebanon and Israel also believed that was his beautiful daughter's dead body," Agude cried out disappointingly.

"Master Agude, the girl got missing for more than seven months. People confessed she died in the forest. By the guidance of our ancestors, gods and God the Father in heaven, her remains were located and buried. And here you are again with a different story. Any way, what exactly do you say about the remains that were interred?" Ayasa asked him with reduced interest.

"I said it already that the remnants were of a chimpanzee," he emphasised.

"What is a chimpanzee?" Ayasa inquired.

"It is an African animal. It lives and hunts in groups. It belongs to the ape family. The chimpanzee is the most similar animal to human beings," Agude disclosed.

"Did you say it belonged to the ape family?" Ayasa asked with concern.

"Heh! Am I a witness in the box to be crossed examined by you? I told you this is a secret so don't push me to the wall," Agude rebutted.

"This is just a simple question my Lord! I know you've not been to class one but I trust your intelligence," Ayasa flattered him.

Agude's head got swollen by his wife's sycophancy and he continued to explain things to her vividly.

"An ape is a large monkey without a tail. It can stand straight and walk on two legs like a human being." Agude stood up and started displaying how chimpanzees walk.

After resuming his seat, he continued by saying that the common apes are the chimpanzees and the gorillas.

Ayasa, who was then concentrating on peeling her cassava for the evening meal warned Agude not to pronounce what he was asserting to anybody anywhere. On one hand, she knew very well that if Agude should utter those words somewhere, he would be fined heavily by the chief and his subjects. It is an indictment on their integrity. On the other hand, Ayasa knew Agude of his cock and bull stories whenever he was having his head in the clouds. But Agude won't shut up. "A chimpanzee was buried like a queen. I won't say this again." Childishly, he used his index finger to seal his mouth like a class one boy. Ayasa packed her things and left for the kitchen. At least that would restrain Agude from saying the dangerous things he was letting loose.

Agude was disappointed. He thought at least his wife would accept this evidence and that would alleviate his worries so he could rest the case but she didn't. Rather, she warned him to shut his gob. Agude continued talking to himself even after his wife left the scene.

"I said this the very night they brought the remains but nobody took me serious. Nobody gives ear to whatever I say in this village. Is it because I am poor? Some people call me Agude, the hopeless pauper. A poor man also has something valuable but people don't know. The people of Owle only listen and accept pointless ideas and arguments from the so called strong and rich people. Though I am poor, I had the gift of discernment from the gods. Time will tell! Anyone who doubts my submission on the interred bones should go to Benin to consult the great oracle, Ordago for the truth. They will surely hear the truth and on that day, Agude will be vindicated," Agude resigned.

Chapter Seventeen

Abrokwa lamented so much over what happened to Sefakor as a result of his love letter to her. He thought seriously about the punishment meted out to her after she was caught reading the love letter in class. He was worried about Sefakor's subsequent dismissal from the school, which was followed by her radical exit from the village leading to her untimely death. The recollection of these line of events increased Abrokwa's troubles and pains. He experienced daunting nightmares, sleepless nights and rejected food for days.

"If Sefakor really ended her life, by committing suicide or perished in the claws of a dangerous animal, then it was all because of my love letter. How can I live and be eating salt and sugar whilst Sefakor is dead and gone. This is unthinkable!" Abrokwa thought seriously about all this.

One night, Abrokwa woke up to pass water when he heard a song from wake keepers from a far away nearby village.

> *The time is ripe,*
> *Lovers are on their way going.*
> *Let's prepare and go with them.*
> *Let's hasten and leave for home.*
> *The home wind is blowing,*

Love Me to the End

Let's hurry up and join our dear ones,
Before darkness sets in.
Verily, verily, we shall meet them.
Meet them at the bank of river Jordan.

The tune and lyrics of the song worked tremendously on Abrokwa's emotions. The day he planned the letter and how he wrote it swirled his mind. He had live and coloured reflection of that day. He then saw Sefakor clearly in his mind's picture. It was as if he was having a cogent vision. Abrokwa saw Sefakor with a small load on her head. She was in a pure white garment, heading towards a destination of no return. It then dawned on him that committing suicide would enable him meet Sefakor's spirit on her way before she crossed to the other side of the river to the home of ancestors. "The earlier I joined her, the better for me," he settled. It was believed that forty days after the funeral of a deceased person, the spirit leaves this world completely for its final home.

Quickly, Abrokwa looked for a strong woven rope that could help him eliminate his life through hanging. The following day at dawn Abrokwa woke up and took the rope. He created a strong loop with a hard knot. He went to the outskirts of the village to finish himself off before people would wake up. He went to the place where people claimed they saw Sefakor for the last time before her exit from the village. An idea came to him that he must bid Apati farewell before his departure to the ancestral world. He therefore decided to go to his friend's house that dawn. Of course, he went there to inform his bosom friend about his decision to kill himself and to bid him goodbye.

Abrokwa quietly sneaked into Apati's house, entered his room and started speaking on top of his voice.

"Apati, Apati, in fact, I cannot continue with life. It is better for me to join Sefakor at where she is before it is too late to meet her," he told Apati in bitter language. At first, Apati heard the words in his dream before he woke up to see Abrokwa beside his mat.

"Abrokwa, how are you going to do this?" Apati questioned him grudgingly from his half sleep.

"You will definitely hear of it when it is accomplished. I am only here to bid you goodbye. Else, I would have met her already by this time of the day," he reiterated.

"Do you mean you want to take your own life?" he asked him sternly.

"Look, it has been said time and again that when the die is cast, no amount of witchery or prayers can obstruct the crossing of the Rubicon. The die is now cast and my journey on this earth has come to an abrupt end. I have no better alternative than to hang myself. My death must follow that of Sefakor as a matter of natural order," Abrokwa assured his friend.

Apati told Abrokwa that his death could not be beneficial to any individual or group of persons. He advised him to rescind his decision and allow the two of them time to look for a better alternative to the problem. "Suicide is never a better choice," Apati convinced him.

Love Me to the End

Apati reminded Abrokwa of a Bible lesson they learnt at school in those days, which indicated that those who died through suicide would never see God. They will rather go to hell where fire will burn them for ever and ever.

"Abrokwa, take heart! If the night is threatening, remember that every cloud has a silver lining. Know that the Almighty in His own wisdom can gild this dark cloud hovering over your head. As times role past; definitely, the gods of Owle will elevate good thoughts in our heads that will lead us into discovery of Sefakor. At that time, silver bright clouds will linger around you and the reflection will be on me. God's ways are not our ways. Let's bank our hopes on Him. Wipe your tears and let's think about a good plan that would be beneficial to you, me and Sefakor's family," Apati landed calmly.

Abrokwa who listened to his friend critically began to see reason. His heart was a bit settled and he could see beyond the ebony dark horizon that seemed to have no light beyond it.

Abrokwa gave up his plans of committing suicide. He deserted the rope in Apati's room and left for home and slept.

Chapter Eighteen

The day broke and the hassles of it began. Abrokwa woke up from his sleep and went back to Apati's house. Apati was his last hope in life. Truly, a friend in need is a friend indeed.

When Abrokwa met Apati, he questioned him about the word 'discovery' he used when he was advising him at dawn. Apati explained his idea behind the discovery of Sefakor. Abrokwa questioned his friend whether to discover Sefakor dead or alive. Apati told Abrokwa that an old man still insisted that the skeletal bones interred in the name of Sefakor were of a big monkey but not of a human being as perceived. Though Abrokwa accepted this with a grain of salt, it gave him some level of vim and vigour that he could see Sefakor some day, some time, somewhere.

Hours rolled by and day light gave way to dusk. After taking his supper, Abrokwa went to bed quietly. He had a lot of dreams that night. In one of the dreams, he met Sefakor and Sefakor told him that she was not dead, but alive. According to her, she was living in an anthill somewhere. This anthill was hiding in a deep forest thousands of miles away from Owle. In this dream, Sefakor did not allow Abrokwa to draw close to her.

In fact, Abrokwa was not happy about how Sefakor prevented him from getting closer to her. Again, he was frightened by the manner in which Sefakor was dressed.

This made Abrokwa wake from his sleep prematurely around 12.00 midnight. After some time, he went back to bed and had another set of dreams. This time round, he met Sefakor again and she proved to him that she was not dead but alive on an unknown land. The next morning Abrokwa narrated all the dreams to his friend Apati. Apati told Abrokwa that he had a similar dream that same night. In his dream, Sefakor told him that she was living under a big community tree in the middle of a small village in the Republic of Benin.

The two bosom friends now got confused and did not know what to do by this development. In their dreams, where Sefakor revealed herself to them, she gave them different places where she was living. That puzzled them about the validity of their dreams. Of course, the same person could not live in an anthill in a thick forest and at the same time at the middle of a village in Benin. If that were true, then she was living as a spirit but not as a mortal being. They tried to wed the two dreams to see the way forward, but that was seemingly unproductive. Finally, they decided to consult a soothsayer. He would weigh the authenticity of their visions and tell them what the future held for them.

The following day, Abrokwa and Apati walked to a village called, Afakorpe, which was seven miles away from Owle. That was where a popular, old fetish priest, Bullamla dwelled. When they went, Bullamla told them to come back after the seventh day. When coming, they should come along with seven eggs, seven cowries and a white dove with a coin that bore a portrait of the head of

Osagyefo Dr Kwame Nkrumah, the first President of the Republic of Ghana. A white piece of cloth and one dress of Sefakor or her photograph or both should be added to the things.

They managed to gather all the items except Sefakor's dress. That was very hard to come by. It was difficult for them to obtain it. This was because anybody in the village who should hear of this would conclude that they had a hand in her death. And they were looking for a way of pacifying her spirit: stopping her ghost from haunting them.

One night, Abrokwa gathered courage and went to Sefakor's house in the night daringly to pick one of her dresses that her mother dried that evening but could not retrieve it as a result of an unexpected downpour. This cloudburst sent people to their beds prematurely that evening. Unfortunately, the dress he picked was not for Sefakor but it was rather for Daada. It was the following morning that he realised that his attempt failed but they did not give up. They needed the dress by all means.

One evening, it dawned on Apati and Abrokwa to go and look for Sefakor's dress at *asadiadome*. That was a small reserved forest, where the people of Owle used to gather property of accident victims for their spirits to come and collect and use. *Asadiadome* was an abominable forest where ordinary people never visited except medicine men. People used to say one could meet ghosts in that forest face to face. Abrokwa and Apati never approached that forest in their life time. Surely, Sefakor belongings; including some of her dresses were dumped in that forest after her burial. It was obvious that it was only at *asadiadome* that Apati and Abrokwa could find Sefakor's dress. There was no way they could send any spiritual man there.

They thought about this for few days and finally decided to go to the forest themselves as the days the medicine man gave them were running out. One night, they prepared; took a torch light and set off to the dangerous forest. A lot of unusual cries from unknown beings scared them but they did not retreat. Finally, they entered the forest and went through the heap of items belonging to dead people. Luckily, after sometime, they got to Sefakor's school uniform and tried to pick it. Apati was more courageous, therefore, he was the one who picked the dress. The dress was wet and heavy but he forced and pulled it out of the items placed on it. Suddenly, Apati felt something long and heavy struggling in the dress. It was a huge snake with a very big head: the type that could swallow a day old baby. Out of fear and wicked bravery, Apati shook the dress with all his strength and the snake fell off with heavy bump on the ground. He held the dress tightly and the two of them took to their heels. They ran very fast without looking back. The snake did not remain there. It cried like a human being and chased them terribly. But it could not catch up with them. They ran for hours without resting on the way until they reached home with the dress.

The following morning, they gathered all the items and took them to the spiritualist. They told him that their priority was to ascertain whether Sefakor was dead or

Love Me to the End

alive. Bullamla collected the items and led them into a small thatch hut. There, the man authorized them to remove all their dresses including their panties. He told both of them to sit on the bare floor. This was difficult for them to do but they obliged. Shortly, Bullamla began performing his assignment. At first, he tried to invite Sefakor's spirit from among the dead to speak to them about where exactly she died and what killed her. He invited the *kutsiami*, the chief of the ancestral world, to bring Sefakor to enable him chat with her.

Kutsiami was responsible for receiving the dead who just crossed the big river and arrived at the ancestral world. He used to receive them by offering them cold, drinking water. After that he would provide them temporal accommodation. He would later look for their relatives for them to give them permanent settlement provided they were good people on earth prior to their demise.

The honourable man went through his records and sent a word to the medicine man that Sefakor was not with them. He told him to rather look for her on the land of the living. He however added that even if Sefakor left the world, her spirit had not yet reached their territory. It would take her forty days to reach their habitat. She warned them that nobody should look for Sefakor among the dead again.

Immediately, the mirror from which the diviner was communicating with the *kutsiami* fell from his grips and got broken into pieces. This stopped Bullamla from further investigations.

Bullamla did not give up. He consulted his oracles to tell exactly where Sefakor could be located in this world. The oracles gave mixed reports about where exactly Sefakor could be found in the world. Nevertheless, it was faintly clear from the divergent submissions that Sefakor was not dead but alive. However, there was no way anybody could meet her. Apart from that she would never return to Owle till her death. "Yes, nobody from your village could see her anywhere again," the oracle reiterated.

The diviner, Bullamla asked Abrokwa and his friend Apati to relax and forget about Sefakor because she would never return. They were, however, bucked up to continue praying for her by pouring libation with white corn flour solution to enable her have a safe stay at her unknown destination. He told them to do this whenever they remembered her.

They continued to question the fetish priest about the perceived skeleton of Sefakor, which was interred. To this, Bullamla said his oracles reported the issue to him one evening that the people of Owle buried a skeleton of a chimpanzee, which died in a forest a decade ago. He told Abrokwa and Apati that there was no need for them to worry their heads again over that issue. "To be frank, the skeleton was that of a chimpanzee. It was never of a human being," he concluded.

Chapter Nineteen

Abrokwa and Apati headed home after consulting the oracle. They believed some of the things Bullamla told them and doubted the rest. After all, they were there when a Catholic Bishop preached one day that fetish priests did tell lies. They believed that Sefakor was alive as pronounced by the diviner but doubted that she could never be seen by anybody. The duo agreed that the latter was a fallacy that should not be bought.

"Why should this man collect all these things from us and later deceive us?" Abrokwa asked Apati defiantly.

"Leave him; he is a wicked, greedy, lazy man. He lacks simple knowledge in human psychology. You don't collect money from someone and tend to tell him what would not make him happy," Apati exclaimed with disappointment.

They both decided that they would look for Sefakor everywhere under the sun. They would move from east to west, north to south. They would travel on foot as far as to the bank of River Jordan. If Sefakor was dead and buried too, they vowed to meet her real grave some day, sometime, somewhere.

Abrokwa and Apati planned their journey in search of Sefakor. Nonetheless, where to pass and where to go was not yet known to them. East, West, North or South, which was the direction to take? They were aware in their Geography lessons at school that the world was round and spherical. Therefore, should they start from the east; they would definitely end in the east through the west. If they should go round the entire world, from the south, it would end in the south through the north. By these calculations they had only two options to take: to the east or the south. But that was still a problem.

They now remembered that they had to pray to the gods to ask them of direction before setting off. They looked for a calabash and corn flour and poured libation. Right after the prayer, they saw a white dove that flew and hovered over their heads directly; flapping its wings and flew towards the eastern part of the village. It followed the path on which people claimed they saw Sefakor for the last time. They concluded that the sunrises from the east and every successful journey starts from the east. So do other good things come from the east. The rising sun would be their guide during the day and the moon and stars shall continue with them during the night. They asked the gods of Owle to be a pillar of cloud to lead them during the dangerous hunt.

With a calabash, gari and sugar as food, a catapult each, small stones, two cutlasses and two gourds of water, they left the village at dawn.

The two strong young men of nineteen: Abrokwa and Apati travelled through thick forests, climbed mountains and descended into deep valleys for several days but did not hear or see the footprints of Sefakor anywhere. They whistled on high mountains with the mind that Sefakor would hear their voices in the valley and respond to them. But all these efforts proved futile.

Finally, they became very tired and weary. Their food got finished, likewise their drinking water. They were now depending on forest wild fruits for food and water from impure streams. They did not have enough of these because sometimes they walked for several miles without coming across a fruit tree or stream. The hamattan just set in and many streams dried up and trees that were not at the bank of a river withered. They now started lamenting seriously about the troubles in which they found themselves. This made Abrokwa regard himself as a man of unfortunate fate. He remembered one of the poems he learnt from his grandmother. Quickly, he wore the poem like a dress that fit him.

> *I know I am a stranded being,*
> *No-one needs to remind me.*
> *People's precious things,*
> *Do remain desolate without protection.*
> *I want to hide under a shady tree,*
> *So the downpour could spare me.*
> *Though I hide under shady trees,*
> *The rain still beats me mercilessly.*
> *Tell that hunter; I am in the forest howling.*
> *Hunter, don't set your gun on me.*
> *I am roaming in the forest.*
> *I am already a distressed animal.*
> *Hunter, don't try your gun on me.*

Immediately Abrokwa started reciting the poem, Apati's mind travelled afar and trickled down on the last days of his deceased grandmother. At the point of her death there was no helper to even fetch water for her to quench her thirst. This innocent old woman was branded a witch. And she was left to suffer an unfortunate fate till her death. This poem was the song she sang till her demise.

The poem made Apati very sad and he pitied Abrokwa seriously. He saw the end of the road as Abrokwa displayed extreme signs of despair and hopelessness. The day Abrokwa gave the letter to him to be given to Sefakor flipped through his mind. He was confident that he Apati had a hand in his friend's predicament. If he were not to give the letter to Sefakor, things wouldn't have gone that way for both of them. This cap fitted him so he wore it.

"Had I known is always at last. If it were today, I wouldn't have made the mistake of giving the letter to Sefakor. But what has no remedy must be without regard. The harm had already been caused," Apati thought.

Owing to this reflection, Apati became silent for a long time. When he broke his silence, he spoke words of encouragement to Abrokwa. This was what he always did throughout all these hard times. He told Abrokwa that the journey was not over yet, therefore, he should not give up entirely. There was still hope for them. Abrokwa was happy that his friend had that kind of bravery, despite the bleakness of their course. He girdled up his loins and they continued the journey without looking back.

Chapter Twenty

One day, Abrokwa and Apati had to spend the night in a thick forest. This forest was so dark that they could not continue with the journey as a result of poor visibility. There was no moon in the sky, which rays could penetrate the thick foliage of the giant, old forest trees. This made the forest terribly dark.

Abrokwa and Apati saw a cave and entered it to see if they could spend the night there safely. After inspection, they saw that the cave was the domicile of a wild animal. It could be for either a tiger or a lion. Despite this hazardous observation, the boys had no alternative than to pass the night there.

In fact, a misfortune that shoves a man does not direct him as to the side of body on which to land. If you are faced with some kind of situation in this life there is no way you will have the opportunity to pause and think of the consequences of any dire action of yours. Whether life or death, lies in the hands of one's fate. This was what hardened Abrokwa and Apati's heart to pass the night in this dangerous cave but with wobbled equilibrium.

The two boys cleared the cave of rotten bones; picked some leaves and laid them on the floor. After that they used their sacks as pillows and slept. Although they gathered the courage to pass the night in the den, they did not lose sight of the fact that anything could happen thereafter. They knew very well that the owner could return at any hour of the night. They were therefore on the red alert so they could not be taken unawares at any part of the night. The wild animal, which dwelled in the cave was not the only predicament. Hunters hunt in the forest at night. Any of them could mistaken them for wild animals and shoot them in the cave. This and the aforementioned made them cover the cave in which they slept with a big stone before sleeping. This action was to prevent any evil that could befall them.

It was not long before they heard of a gunshot far away in the forest. It was a hunter who shot an animal. Perhaps, the bullets did not hit the animal properly and could thus not kill the animal in question.

"Yes, a strolling hunter and a strolling animal had met somewhere," Abrokwa told Apati in a funny way.

The animal that was shot ran at a very fast speed through the forest. Abrokwa and Apati could hear the sound of its footsteps on dry leaves from afar. The sound drew close and closer to them. Shockingly, the speed finally withered at the doorway of the cave where they were hiding. The wounded animal struggled to enter but it couldn't make it. It couldn't have the opportunity to enter because the gate was closed. The animal therefore decided to sleep at the entrance. After all, if you have trouble in town and you are wise, you have to go back home. That was exactly what the animal did. The animal lay there, groaning in pain from the bullet wounds. It was deprived of its place of abode by an unknown assailant: of course, another human being. This animal was very unlucky that night. It had a double agony to ponder over that cold hamattan night. Had I known, is always at last. If it had known, it wouldn't have left the cave that night at all.

Abrokwa and Apati woke up and peeped through the sides of the stone they used in blocking the gate of the cave. There lay a wild, big, old, wounded lion. Blood was oozing from its claws and nostrils profusely. Its eyes were stuck open with terror. One could read a high degree of rage and bitterness unfolding from its eye balls. The sight of the lion frightened them and they were filled with concentrated nervousness. The wounded lion snarled and its canines were glaringly exposed – revealing signs of possible revenge at the least opportunity. It was really a terrifying scene to witness.

Abrokwa and Apati slept stiffly, as if they were dead bodies. They made sure the lion did not get any signal that the human being who wounded it has his children in its den. Should that happen, then it would become a do and die affair. The lion could do all it would take to devour them either for food or for revenge or both. If the lion was not able to roll the stone, then it would remain there until they made the attempt to escape. Several thoughts dripped into their minds one after the other.

Definitely, Abrokwa and his friend would not remain in the lion's grotto for more than twenty four hours. The ventilation in the cavern was very poor. They would be hungry and would have to come out to look for food. They would be thirsty and have to look for water to drink. They would have to attend nature's call. Above all, they have to continue with their search for Sefakor. Therefore, they could not remain in that dangerous dungeon. These thoughts coupled with others made them keep vigil. They could not sleep throughout the night. The lion also could not sleep due to the   pains from the wounds it sustained from the bullets. The anxiety to enter into its den which was occupied by an unknown stranger was equally a source of worry to the lion. It groaned in pain as it rolled from side to side till daybreak.

As of 9.00 am the next day, the lion did not go for break for Apati and Abrokwa to flee. Apati spotted the lion, which was now lying quietly as a result of a little relief. He saw that it was badly wounded. He then whispered to Abrokwa: "This lion cannot kill any human being due to how the bullets destroyed its claws. Let's gather courage and go out. After all, if it can catch at all, not both of us at once." He told Abrokwa that they could defend themselves with their hands and catapults if the lion should make any attempt to catch any of them. He reminded him of the story of Sampson in the Bible, who killed lions with his hands. "After all, Agbematsi, my great grandfather used to kill wild animals with his hands and teeth," he emphasized.

Obviously, Abrokwa did not support Apati's babyish suggestions. He saw that his friend was underrating the strength of the lion. He reminded him of the speed at which the lion ran before getting to the cave. "Look, the race of life is not taken with reluctance. If death should appear, the cripple will also do his best to escape before he would be reached," he assured Apati.

Abrokwa prolonged jogging Apati's memory. He told him that if a pig's face is covered with mud, its eyes are never covered. Already, the lion was hungry and could not go anywhere for food. Hence, if they should come out, it would definitely catch one of them for food. He reminded his friend that the lion was aware that it was a human being who wounded it. Any encounter with a human being at that juncture would be a do and die affair for it.

Apati saw reason but did not stop looking for the alternative approach. He quickly refined his thinking cap for a different idea. He told Abrokwa: "There is none that eats flesh that nothing eats its flesh. There is none that devours that nothing can devour. This dreadful lion you see there, fears something in life by all means."

Abrokwa told Apati that he got it wrong. "Vultures eat flesh but nothing eats their flesh," Abrokwa reminded Apati.

Apati did not surrender. He told Abrokwa that it was a man who wounded the lion, for that reason, it would habour an instinct of fear within it for man. "We must be bold to make it aware that it is we human beings who are occupying his den. The gun that wounded it is the same gun that we are carrying," Apati proclaimed.

Apati gathered more vim and vigour as he saw that Abrokwa was giving ear to his submissions. He reiterated that if the lion was not courageous and his guess was right, then it would run away when they revealed themselves. "Let us make a loud, careless noise and catapult it incessantly and see if it will not run away? Without this, we shall remain in this cave for days, so long as this lion remains here," Apati rested his case.

Abrokwa now perceived little logic in what Apati was saying. Thus, the two of them agreed on this and planned it tactfully. They made sure the cave was well closed from within. Within the twinkling of an eye, they took their catapults with few marbles and began the onslaught. They targeted the eye of the lion, which was glaring from the cave and hit it concurrently. They shouted at the same time, restlessly like booming bombs. The lion got startled by this out of the blue turn of events. It got scared and jumped on its feet. The lion had no chance to decide what to do. It took to its heels and ran aggressively from the cave till the whole creature shrunk into the thick forest. They heard the sound of its speed till the sound faded completely.

Now, Abrokwa and Apati looked into each other's face and heaved a sigh of relief. They rolled the stone and came out of the cave to continue their journey.

Chapter Twenty-One

Abrokwa and Apati poured libation and thanked the gods for saving them from the claws of the dangerous, wounded lion. After the prayers, they set off. They headed towards the due east. After walking for about two kilometers, they felt very hungry. They cast their eyes through the canopy of the giant trees. They were looking for consumable fruits to assuage their hunger. Like the biblical fig tree, none of the trees around bore fruits at that moment. After surging forward a bit, their eyes caught a glimpse of a big, old mango tree ahead of them. By an act of providence, the kind mango tree beckoned them to come around and eat. The action of the tree was analogous to what their mothers used to do for them when they were still minors. Their mothers on Saturday mornings used to invite them to come and eat quickly so they could leave for farm.

They focused their eyes on the mango tree and could picture hundreds of very juicy mangoes on top of this benevolent tree. They thanked their stars and waded through the forest towards the foster mother's kitchen. Within the shortest possible time, they were under the tree. Hastily, Apati climbed the tree and shook one of its branches with the rest of his energy. A lot of mangoes fell on the ground for them. They gobbled and crunched these mangoes to their satisfaction.

Love Me to the End

During the meal, Abrokwa remembered Sefakor seriously and said "Apati, if Mother Nature can whisper to me the whereabouts of Sefakor, I shall keep one pretty, juicy mango for her. I shall give it to a loving, heavenly bird to fly to her. Maybe, she may be hungry like we were. She will use this to remember me."

Apati lauded Abrokwa's intentions. Quickly, he pointed a finger at one beautiful, soft, round mango and said: "Abrokwa, that is the one you will send to her if wishes were horses."

"When shall wishes become horses in this stringent world of ours?" Abrokwa questioned.

After eating the mangoes, they carried a few of the fruits in their small sacks and set off again. They were not yet at the end of the journey, therefore, there was no time to waste. There were three things ahead of them. Seeing Sefakor face to face; meeting her dead body or the two of them dying to meet Sefakor at the bank of River Jordan.

Although the parents of Abrokwa and Apati were traditional worshippers, the boys had some knowledge of Bible stories. This was so because they studied a bit of Bible Knowledge (B.K) at middle school. The issue of River Jordan got refreshed in their minds when they thought of death. They remembered a song Mr Sapong taught them when they were in class six and they both began singing it slowly. They wouldn't like their voices to be heard from afar. The lion was still in the forest. They sang the song together and moved on its rhythm..

Love Me to the End

Jordan, Jordan, across the Jordan,
We shall see the promised land of honey
We shall meet; we shall see our loved ones
Flowers, flowers around the Jordan
Joy, joy, joy, joy,
There, joy shall never end.

This was an old school song they used to sing during their school days whenever a colleague passed on. They sang the song as they climbed a small mountain. This song relieved them from the fatigue of climbing such a mountain. Soon, they were at the peak of the mountain. On the mountain, they saw a river in the valley ahead of them. It was about half a kilometre afar from their location. The river looked like a confluence of River Volta and River Danyi. This at least gave them the fortitude that though they covered a lot of miles in the journey, they were still within the boundaries of West Africa.

They sat on the mountain for a while to take a rest. They observed the scenery and enjoyed the panorama of the flowering trees along the banks of the rivers. Nonetheless, the beauty of the landscape could not hold them there for long. They had a task on hand to accomplish. They jumped onto their feet and descended the mountain. They moved with vigour towards the rivers. Surprisingly, the closer they got to the confluence, the farther they saw it until the two rivers that merged disappeared completely. They quivered from this great shock. It was like a dream to them. This mystery confused them but they did not give up. "Forward ever, backwards never," they conferred.

They stirred up their confidence and surged forward. After some time, they got to a narrow winding path and followed it. Quickly, out of the blue, the path became forked into two. A gentle, soft, cold wind blew rapidly and they were caught up in the cold. The whole weather seemed to be like the season of winter in a foreign country. It was a mark of meeting a group of ancestral spirits. There was no doubt that the latter was in the offing. Abrokwa and Apati got troubled and confused about this wonderful incident. They stood still to assess the situation. Water in form of dawn dews suddenly began dribbling on them. This lasted for some ten seconds.

Abrokwa remembered a dream he had the previous night. He started narrating the dream to Apati. In the dream, they met Sefakor at a junction. She was in a very white garment with golden linen. She looked like a goddess – pure and too holy to approach. Due to this, they could neither touch nor communicate with her. He got dazed and was compelled to resurrect from the dream.

Apati trusted Abrokwa's dreams. He told Abrokwa that if this dream would materialise like other dreams of his then at that juncture, a miracle was imminent. That would be the end of their journey.

"I think that was why the ancestors sprinkled the dews on us," Apati registered blissfully.

They did not move from that spot before a strange stench engulfed them. Apati whose father was a very powerful man; a man of many spirits acknowledged the scent. He told his friend that the stench was coming from a group of dwarfs. He said dwarfs could be on parade somewhere in the forest. The scent was meant to drive away any human being that was likely to get closer to their assembly. Apati looked on the ground and he spotted a string of a long single hair on the floor. He picked it up elegantly. "This belongs to a dwarf," Apati said. "Could it be that they have been taking care of Sefakor for all these months?" Abrokwa asked.

"If we do not retreat by returning to where we were coming from, we will vanish and no one can trace us," Apati warned. To Abrokwa's surprise, Apati started speaking as if a spirit had possessed him in the wake of his last words. "If we don't leave this place we shall get missing right now," Apati reiterated in a funny babyish voice.

The joy of meeting Sefakor pretty soon changed to a different nightmare. Apati started behaving strangely. Abrokwa did not understand this phenomenon. He got confused and did not know what to do. They did not intend to return home without meeting Sefakor. Moving forward was nevertheless suicidal and moving back was a blot on their integrity. Standing still could mean a dangerous scenario. However, in this state of dilemma, they had no alternative than to remain at where they were already standing. They stood there sheepishly. They were caught in the web of a disaster. They remained there as stiff as deadwood.

Out of the blue, they heard the voice of an old man approaching. They were a bit relieved. Perhaps, the gods had realised their predicament and sent someone to rescue them – they thought. To their surprise, they saw a very short and dumpy man with very long grey hair. This man was not bearing features of a normal human being. And they saw another one of the same stature following the first one. And then another one of different colour advanced towards the first two. At last, Abrokwa and Apati saw a host of them in full glare, jostling their way through the forest. They were all having very bushy hair, which saw no pair of scissors or shaving blade in their life time. They were moving in a straight queue, as if they were on a school parade. They were surging forward, yet their feet were facing the opposite direction. The tallest was at the height of the size-thirty bucket.

All those who were in front were like typical black people from Africa. And those behind looked superior to those in front. They were like people from the advanced world: Europe and America. The latter appeared more furious, wild and wicked. Typically, they were commanders over those in front of them.

"Dwarfs!" Apati shouted to Abrokwa who was yet to see them clearly. That marked the end of the period the two boys thought normally as human beings. They were in a trance – dazed and transposed into a world of unconsciousness.

The dwarfs carried the boys to a huge anthill deeper in the forest. This anthill was one of the anthills in which the dwarfs lived. This particular anthill was where they used to quarantine human beings and other creatures that strayed into their way. It was like a dungeon, where dwarfs kept recalcitrant people and other disobedient spirits.

Abrokwa and Apati were kept in this anthill for four solid weeks. Should they remain there for forty days, then they would turn into permanent immortals. They would become permanent spiritual servants for the dwarfs. And that would be the end of their journey. Probably, they could continue searching for Sefakor in the spiritual realm in case they would still perceive things the same way when they were normal human beings.

The first thing the dwarfs did was to change their names. They called Abrokwa Mimi and Apati, Pupu. Mimi and Pupu were so obedient to the dwarfs. Their meekness paid off after the thirtieth day, thus, they were set free. The dwarfs carried them to the same spot where they carried them. That was when they came back to their natural senses by regaining their composure.

Throughout the period that Abrokwa and Apati were with the dwarfs, they were served with no food apart from bananas and *lififli* – food prepared from corn flour and palm oil.

The dwarfs did not just set the boys free but they gave them series of punishments. This was a normal thing dwarfs used to do to men and creatures who got into their way. They punished them because they shouldn't have ventured into their track. They punished them by giving them twenty lashes each and then little kindness. On that hour, they took them to a big laboratory to train them as pharmacists. In fact, no human being can tell exactly where this lab is situated in this world, though it existed. They taught them how to communicate with plants that have medicinal potency. "If someone is sick and you get to the bush, plants that can cure the sickness will beckon you to come to them. Boldly ask them to direct you as to how to use them and what sickness to use them for. Your presence in this great laboratory, coupled with the powers we are giving to you, the plants will tell you exactly what to do," the dwarf scientist told them.

The dwarfs taught them some herbs that could heal any human being even at the point of death. After all this, they warned them to go home straight and not to remain in the forest again. "We shall finish you, if we should meet you somewhere in the forest again. Your friends and relatives would not see where you will be buried," the chief dwarf warned them.

Chapter Twenty-Two

It was one Sunday evening. A thick cloud of smoke swirled and hovered over the entire village of Tufiakwa. Hundreds of insects and animals were seen escaping the wrath of the wildfire. The scenario became horrifying when poisonous snakes crisscrossed paths of the village and sought refuge in people's bedrooms.

Water which people stored in barrels and big pots got finished as men and women busily poured out all drops including dregs on the thatch roofs. Their motive was to wet the roofs before the fire jettisoned its red tongues into the village. They detected ahead of time that the fire may like to lick rooftops and descend into rooms to consume valuable property including human beings.

Many men and women dashed to streams and well sides to draw more water to the village before the fire made an attempt to destroy the village. "Ready for war, war never takes one at a disadvantage," was the old adage. The people of Tufiakwa were not expecting the fire, hence, they were taken unawares. This was not the first time fire invaded the village. Nonetheless, the current one was a bolt from the blue and was extremely dreadful.

Liwabi in the morning returned from the distant forest where he sent food to the perceived goddess, Sefakor.

That morning, he had a game: a very fat grasscutter. His wife pounded fufu for the whole family. The goddess in the forest equally had a good share of the meal. In fact, that evening was more than a golden jubilee for Sefakor. She enjoyed the food and drank the sweet palm-wine, which was added to the meal.

Apparently, it was only mother God who did know that was the last meal from Sefakor's benefactor to her.

As a matter of fact, for the six years that Liwabi served the goddess in the forest, his destiny changed. His economic conditions got better by the minute of the hour. He became a prosperous hunter overnight. Hunting became a very lucrative venture to him. He got antelopes, grasscutters, porcupines and other animals whenever he went out hunting. For rats, squirrels, bats and partridges, he got a good number almost every day. The situation appeared as if a benevolent spirit drove animals and birds into his tracks. Of course, success smiled at him broadly. This was however not the same with other veteran hunters in the village.

Liwabi sold game almost every day to both indigenes and strangers. 'Chopbar' operators in big towns and cities traced him to Tufiakwa to buy game. People confessed that the soup prepared from Liwabi's game and the meet were so palatable that 'chopbar' operators who bought game from him made a lot of food sales day by day. Hence, their customers shifted from buying food from other people. Their food was ordered in large quantities for very important people like government officials. As a result of this, traders used to dash Liwabi money on several occasions in order to win his favour.

By chance, by faith or by mere coincidence, Sefakor brought good luck to Liwabi and his household. Of course, this was what sustained his interest in taking care of the goddess all these years without getting tired of it.

Sefakor lived well in the heart of this deadly forest for years. Her benefactor did all he could to make her have her breakfast and supper every blessed day. Sefakor never lacked water nor food throughout the period. Sometimes, during festivals Liwabi used to add soft drinks and sweet palm-wine to her meals. Other items Sefakor could use were equally provided occasionally. Clothing, pomade, comb, powder and others were provided. Thus, Sefakor never regretted running away from Owle, except for the fact that she dearly missed her family members and the boy who proposed love to her.

The wildfire now drew closer to the village. It was in the dry season and most of the leaves and grasses had withered and were dried up. Owing to this, any little wind that blew made the fire travel at a great speed.

The fire got close to the village now and was about to befriend the thatch roofs. It would first do that to those on the outskirts before extending the handshake to those at the middle of the village, if the chance were there.

Quickly, the fire pierced its red tongue back and forth as if it was only interested in licking the apex of the roofs. Men in the village disagreed with this bastard fire. They got into more action; fighting it with the rest of their energy and might. They fought the wicked fire fearlessly. But the fire became more notorious and very recalcitrant. The flames raged and surged forward dangerously into the village as a gallant warrior who feared no bullet. The smoke darkened the whole atmosphere; conjuring an eclipse of the sun into being. Visibility became very poor. Men could not stand the horror, yet they did not intend to allow the fire to persist. The fire crackled laughter on seeing the men as mere jokers who did not know what was ahead of them. All too soon, the men started retreating as the flames of the fire shoved them with impunity.

It was not human beings alone who were at risk. Snakes, scorpions and other dangerous creatures were equally in danger. Snakes escaping the fire strayed into the village, increasing the woes of men. People unknowingly began stepping on the dangerous reptiles. The snakes retaliated by biting the people. The people of Tufiakwa experienced double agony. They were confronted with the wrath of the bushfire and the venom from the terrified snakes and scorpions. The people now thought it wise to escape from the wildfire, snakes and scorpions by moving out of the village. Nonetheless, the time that decision disembarked was too late. Where to pass to escape the trouble was a problem as the fire already engulfed the entire village.

A serious calamity befell Tufiakwa on that day and there was no chance for the inhabitants to pause and think about the solution, which could never be fetched at that crucial moment. Amidst wails and cries, people hopelessly darted helter-skelter for their precious lives.

Parents forget about their children as it came to everybody for himself, God for us all.

Almost the whole village got into flames and within three hours the entire village was razed down to ashes. Men, women, and children like fatherless ants; without protection, perished in the wildfire. The only person who survived the disaster was an old woman who was branded a witch and was cast out of Tufiakwa and settled in a far away village. She was the only indigenous person who was not at home before the disaster struck.

Late in the afternoon, Liwabi took his gun to go and kill some squirrels in the forest. Liwabi saw the flames when he was going and returned home to save his wife and children. The fire took him at a disadvantage as he returned to the village at the spur of the moment. Immediately Liwabi entered the house for action, the fire ringed the entire village and consumed everything including him and his household.

One night, Sefakor had a dream and met Liwabi face to face. He brought her food to her as usual. In the dream Liwabi drew closer to Sefakor for the first time and conversed with her fondly. During the conversation, Sefakor told Liwabi her total story. She told him about what brought her to the heart of that forest. Liwabi then promised to bring her to the village to live with him and his family, once she was a human being like them. He told Sefakor in the dream that he would give his eldest son to her to marry. Though Sefakor was happy about leaving the forest to the village, she was not enthused over the idea of marrying Liwabi's son. This was because Abrokwa still occupied her mind and she could not love any man apart from him who wrote her the letter of her peril.

Liwabi and Sefakor did not settle on the proposal before Liwabi left her as if he was responding to an emergency call. Before leaving, he told Sefakor that his days were numbered and if they did not meet again, then they would meet after death. He bade her farewell and was about to leave. Suddenly, a wild animal spitting out fire appeared. This animal roared like a lion and hurled fire at Liwabi from its mouth. The fire rapidly consumed Liwabi completely in the presence of Sefakor. This scared Sefakor in the dream terribly.

Sefakor cried bitterly in the nightmare as she knew definitely that the death of Liwabi, her benefactor could mean her death was equally imminent. Immediately, she woke up to notice that it was just one of those bad dreams she used to have. She was relieved from the trauma when she realised that it was a dream after all.

The morning sprang in and Sefakor woke up expecting her food and water as usual but nothing came forth. She did not hear from anybody from far away fields as it used to be. And for the whole day nothing was brought to her by Liwabi. She was consequently compelled by the circumstances to starve for the whole day. She had no water to drink, no food to eat and no water to bath.

The following day too, nothing came. Sefakor now set out to go and look for some fruits to eat. That morning, she gathered water from night dews, which settled on the broad leaves. She got little water from the leaves to at least quench her thirst.

Sefakor was not able to go far away from her abode as she did not know even the first environment near her place of settlement very well. She developed the instinct that she might lose her way and get missing. Therefore, she only roamed the forest few metres around her home. She did not find any food to eat. This time, she became very weak as a result of severe hunger. She decided to withdraw from the forest and go back to her place. She thought before she returned Liwabi would have surfaced with her food and water. That would be for all the days that she did not receive anything from him. He was a kind man and he could settle all the arrears. "Maybe, this man travelled and he would return by this time. He will bring to me all he failed to bring to me for the past days," she reflected.

When Sefakor returned, to her surprise, there was no sign of Liwabi and nothing was brought.

Sefakor went back to the forest now a bit deeper and more desperate. She saw a tree which resembled a cassava tree. She approached it and hastily uprooted it. She got two tubers. Quickly, she took one tuber and peeled off the bark with her front teeth. She got to the flesh and began crunching it like a hungry goat devouring cassava leaves. Sefakor swallowed the substance rapidly when she got to know that it was not bitter. A point in time, she discerned that the taste was not that of real cassava but, she had no alternative than to satisfy herself and go her way. Some people hold the belief that if you eat food and feel satisfied and die later, it is better than to remain hungry and be suffering. Sefakor continued chewing and swallowing the perceived cassava until she was fully satisfied. Unfortunately, the root crop was not meant for human consumption. If it should be eaten at all, it should not be eaten raw. The raw one was poisonous for humans and rodents that was why rats, mice and grasscutters never ate it. The people of Tufiakwa did call it *ma2umaku,* meaning let me eat and die.

Within thirty minutes, Sefakor developed stomach aches. The pains were mild from the beginning but later became severe. Sefakor rolled on the ground and cried for help, but there was nobody around to assist her. Sefakor went through this pain for six solid days like a pregnant woman in a tediously protracted labour.

Now, Sefakor became helpless and could not even stand from where she slept. She was just waiting for death to come and carry her away. She was sure that was the end of her life's journey should Liwabi not show up at that critical moment.

Chapter Twenty-Three

Liwabi never came to the forest again. The truth of the matter was that Liwabi lost his life during the fire outbreak, therefore, he was not alive to save Sefakor. Already, as a good father, he appeared to Sefakor in her dream and bade her goodbye. Unless a miracle occurred, the time was ripe for Sefakor to follow Liwabi.

One terrible day, it was obvious that Sefakor would pass on by sunset. Sefakor recounted facts about life and married them with how she was going to die.

"Every living thing dies – birds, animals, trees, plants, insects and human beings of all ages; young and old – even day old babies die.

"At least, I spent some years in this painful world. Leaving for home at this age is not a bad exit once the boat on which I am travelling has hit a rock at the deepest part of the sea. I spent six good years in this forest and the time is ripe for me to leave for my maker's home!" Sefakor reasoned in a worried manner.

Although Sefakor has accepted to die, her worry was how she was going to bury herself in the heart of the desolate forest, where no relative was likely to see her remains. She was going to bury herself as tortoise did.

Sefakor shook her head in dismay and her thoughts flipped her back to Owle. She imagined the kind of burial she would have received if she were to die at Owle. To die at that age would have ripped open the whole village. She descended the vast memory lane and saw that she would have been in lower six as of that age if she stayed at Owle and continued her education to secondary school. She would die as a lower six student. "Eh, sweet lower lady of Ho Mawuli Secondary School – a Mawulian!" she fancied.

That would have shaken the Owle village. She calculated how six formers from various secondary schools in the region would troop into Owle to fill the village to capacity for her burial. They would tie red bands around their wrists, heads and some would use them as belt and neckwear. Yes, sports ladies and gentlemen would display sports skills and gymnastics. And she would be laid in state in a white sparkling gown like a bride waiting for her groom. She imagined how Abrokwa and Apati would slink into the room where her body would be displayed. And Abrokwa would place his hand on her cold chest devastatingly.

Sefakor started crying when she focused once again on how Abrokwa would stand near her body when in state and present a white handkerchief to her as the last gift from his heart. That was the handkerchief she would use to wipe her face on the way to the land of no return.

She pondered over how students would file past her remains step by step, one after the other with the song:

> *God be with you till we meet again.*
> *May He at all times direct you;*
> *May He in life's storm protect you;*

Love Me to the End

God be with you till we meet again
Till we meet, till we meet
Till we meet at Jesus' feet
Till we meet, till we meet
God be with you till we meet again.

There, the register would be marked and her name would be mentioned three times. There would be no response and her name would be removed finally from the school's books.

Then the school band of her middle school would trumpet from the school compound and the pupils would queue in long files on the street for the last respect. And onlookers would be crying from their hearts for the death of a promising, pretty, young lady. Then the school cadet – the military students; selected from form one to form five of Mawuli Secondary School would lift her coffin; raise it and move straight like soldiers, amidst cries and wails from countless sympathisers. She daydreamed of how the coffin would be raised high and be clouded in the family best *kente* cloth. She saw the picture of pretty girls carrying countless wreaths taking the lead with regal steps and choirs following them, and then the brass band in that order. At the thin end of a winding long line, would be a scattered group of people, who would not be able to reach the graveyard. They would have the opportunity to gossip about what had killed such a girl at that prime age.

Sefakor brought to the fore how her mother and her mother's friends would tie their cloths on their bellies and sing sorrowful dirges with rattles and trot in their groups along the narrow streets of Owle. She remembered the song the students would sing before descending the gentle hill into the Evangelical Presbyterian cemetery:

> *How can it be that I should gain*
> *Forgiveness through the saviour's blood?*
> *Died He for me, who caused His pain,*
> *For me, who Him to death pursued?*
> *Amazing love! How can it be*
> *That you my Lord should die for me?*
> *Amazing love! How can it be*
> *That you my Lord should die for me?*

Immediately the casket arrives at the cemetery, the pastor would take over. That would be his last opportunity to pour his final blessings upon her remains. He would fetch the earth, with a shovel at his left and the Bible on the right hand and pour the soil on the coffin three times saying:

"The sun shall no longer be your light by day, nor for brightness shall the moon give light to you. But the Lord will be to you an everlasting light, and your God your glory. Your sun shall no longer go down, nor shall your moon withdraw itself. For the Lord will be your everlasting light. And the days of your mourning shall be ended. Out of the earth you were created and the earth you will turn into. Your deeds shall follow you! Rest in Peace!"

The pastor would then call for the closing hymn. After that guys in the village – Sefakor's relatives and Abrokwa's friends would take over. They would carry their shovels and cover the coffin completely by filling the grave to the brim. They would raise it above ground level, creating a long fruitless mound. What the plant shall never germinate in this world. Groups would lay their wreaths and loved ones would pick forget-me-not flowers and break twigs of hibiscus and bougainvillea and place them on her grave solemnly to indicate their last respect. This is the period the drumming and singing from *borborbor*, *gabada* and *jama* groups would die down: "signifying the end of my era," Sefakor mirrored.

That kind of burial would have been the best for Sefakor. Sweet home going, where in her white beautiful robe with flowers in hand, host of special angels and ancestors would queue to give her a rousing welcome back home. "Daughter of the soil, welcome back home! They would welcome me: yes, they would," Sefakor speculated.

Sefakor's mind lingered in this world; fantasizing her death and burial at Owle as nature pushed her gradually towards her end. Of course, though she would not be accorded that kind of burial, she depended on that nostalgic judgment to slip into the next world painfully. She started burying herself before passing on at last, ushering her body and soul into the hands of her maker.

Out of the blue, birds gathered on top of the tree that served as Sefakor's shelter. Their number on that day was higher than ever. Most of the birds wore black feathers. They started chirping sadly in low unison immediately they gathered. They were not as happy as they used to be. They were singing sorrowful songs persistently as if they were mourning the death of a fellow. "Nature is so wonderful. These birds brought me under this tree and they are here again on my last hour to say farewell to me. They are here to bury me," Sefakor told herself.

The birds, however, changed their mood and song when they pictured two men far way approaching the place. The black ones started disappearing; giving way to those with white feathers to take over. They sang happily a lot of victorious love songs. By the behaviour of these birds, Sefakor discerned that there was joy after death after painful life on earth. "After severe darkness, light will shine on my way," Sefakor wrapped up.

Chapter Twenty-Four

The beatings from the dwarfs were so severe that Abrokwa and Apati could not continue with the journey on that day. They remained under a big tree for three days. On the third day, they woke up and thought seriously about going back home.

The lingering issue was where to pass in order not to get into the hands of the dwarfs again.

Apati reminded Abrokwa that they moved towards the East but did not meet any fortune, therefore, this time round, they should move towards the West. They both agreed on that and walked abreast of each other on the narrow path. Soon, the path diminished and there was no road ahead of them to continue. That was the end of the road. They, therefore, decided to retreat. After studying the path critically, they realised that it was the branches of a fallen tree that blocked it. They consequently struggled through the thick branches of the fallen tree and got into the path and followed it. After an hour, they got to the junction of another forked road. They quickly remembered their encounter with the dwarfs when they reached the same type of forked road. Fear gripped them and they got perplexed. They did not distinguish whether it should be the left or the right. They stood still contemplating over the solution to their tight circumstance. Far away in the forest, they heard some birds chirping sorrowfully. The cries of the birds caught their attention and that gradually increased their state of dilemma. They decided to move towards that direction to observe what was transpiring up there.

As they got closer to the place, the cries of the birds seemed like a cluster of people singing dirges on top of a tree. However, there was no sign that anybody ever lived in that forest that a choir should gather there singing. Again, human beings cannot climb in their numbers to the top of a tree and sing. Therefore, it was clear to them that it was birds whose voices blended into what appeared like a human orchestra.

There was no path to get to where the birds were. Their movement was obstructed by strong, thorny, forest ropes. Some of these ropes were full of wild thorns. Another obstacle was from protruding roots, tree stumps, big trees, rocks and dangerous, deep holes. After a spell of struggling their way through the forest, they got closer to the tree. That was where they heard *akpese* dance-like song clearly.

The birds acknowledged the presence of Abrokwa and Apati. Few minutes after, the birds caught a clear glimpse of them and suddenly changed the music into a triumphant love song. It was as if the birds were now at a wedding ceremony, singing their praise for the freshly wedded couple. As if they were welcoming them, they sang the loudest.

I target you; pretty girl.

Love Me to the End

Tell your parents to keep you for me.
I target you; gentle boy.
Tell your parents to keep you for me.
The day I shall marry you,
The whole world will hear.
All and sundry will hear of it.

Apati and Abrokwa tried to get to the tree but there was no way they could get there. A host of bees emerged and surrounded the area. Although the bees were not wild, Abrokwa and his friend feared to get close to them. That was the decisive point. They felt that was the end of the journey. They have now agreed to go back home after several days of a vain search of a missing darling.

Abrokwa called his friend and said to him; "Apati, I thank you very much for the love you showed me during this difficult moment of my life. A friend in need is really a friend indeed. You displayed to me beyond all doubts that you really love and care for me. You did all you could to assist me unearth Sefakor, but we did not succeed. Our journey is all vanity; a useless expedition. It is as useless as life on earth. As the elders say 'an endless song would only break the rattle.' No condition is permanent and every long way has an end. The end of every road is in the room. Enough is enough! We have suffered a lot on this journey. Thirst and hunger were always with us," Abrokwa gapped.

Abrokwa detailed some of the things they suffered during the journey to his friend. "We passed the night in the den of a wounded lion. Dwarfs carried us away and finally flogged us mercilessly. We are yet to recover from the wounds inflicted on us by the dwarfs. They warned us to leave for home but here we are; still in this wilderness. When darkness falls on you in a forest, you must go back home if you are a wise person. Darkness has fallen on our journey and it's time we gave up and return home. When Sefakor died somewhere, at an unknown destination, may her spirit rest in the hands of Orkatsie Dake and other faithful ancestors of our age. Dake never dies, likewise Onetsie Golo. Our ancestors will be kind enough to offer her cold water to quench her thirst. They will provide her a room to lay her head." After these words, Abrokwa burst into uncontrollable tears. He cried and sobbed like a day old baby.

"Sefakor, Sefakor, we love you, but your creator loves you most. May your soul rest in peace!" Abrokwa was done.

Abrokwa could not stop crying. Ceaseless tears dribbled from his eyes and flowed down his cheeks like a baby looking for its missing mother.

In fact, the tree that Abrokwa and Apati were trying to reach was Sefakor's dwelling place. That was where Sefakor lay helplessly; galloping towards death. Sefakor was left with few seconds to give up the ghost. Sefakor in this state heard a human voice calling her name faintly. But it was like a delusion to her, therefore, she remained silent.

Apati, who stood uncomfortably watching Abrokwa and listening to his sorrowful words realised that the boat really hit a rock. He looked at Abrokwa sternly and felt pity for him. He looked into the sky and thanked the gods for their guidance and protection so far throughout the journey. He now lowered his heard and shouted the name of Sefakor three times as Abrokwa did.

"Sefakor, Sefakor, Sefakor, where are you on this earth? If you are no more among the living, then go and come no more, because the world was too wicked to you. I pray that one day, we shall meet at the big market place, where people go and come to this world no more. If you are really dead, then you should rest quietly. Have nothing against Abrokwa and me who, out of love, caused you all your agonies in this wicked world. As for Mr Boso, and his wicked head teacher, Pataku, when they move in the morning, move with them. When they carry water to drink, poison it with crocodile bile. When they carry food to eat, spit reeking saliva into it. When they drink palm-wine at a funeral, let them remain there for children to whip. When you meet them at a crossroad, axe and maim them."

Sefakor's name, which Apati mentioned with a loud voice sounded in Sefakor's ears like a ringing bell. It then dawned on her that it was Abrokwa's voice that she heard first. She quaked and struggled to stand but that was difficult because of how weak she was. New life came into her and she called back the name of Abrokwa: "Abrokwa, Abrokwa, Abrokwa leeee ..." In fact, Abrokwa did not hear his name being mentioned due to the way the birds were still howling. Apati however heard it but dimly. He told Abrokwa to remain calm – the soothsayer's prophecy and Agude's submissions seemed to come to pass. "What!" Abrokwa asked in astonishment. "What are you saying?" he questioned.

Sefakor called again; this time louder. Abrokwa heard his name clearly from Sefakor. He called her hack:

"Sefakor!"

"Yes, Abrooo, I am here, come!"

"Who are you and where are you?" Abrokwa asked.

"I am Sefakor, your darling girl," responded the voice.

Abrokwa and Apati forgot about the presence of the bees and shot themselves into the thickly enveloped bushes, which wickedly separated them from Sefakor. Each of them would like to be the first to meet her. They were gashed by strong bush thorns but that could not stop them from surging ahead. Finally, they got to the spot where Sefakor lay. There slept Sefakor; wet, weak, frail and helpless – at the point of death. She was astonished and speechless.

Abrokwa and Apati remembered the medicine the dwarfs thought them. They spoke to the leaves, picked those that responded and squeezed their sap into Sefakor's nostrils. Suddenly, Sefakor regained her health and became very strong. Sefakor became strong as if nothing had ever happened to her. Hail and hearty, she hugged Apati gracefully. She then turned to her lover Abrokwa. They embraced each other and kissed fervently. They got glued to each others arms for minutes. It was like a dream to all of them. Of course, it was a big dream that materialised. Abrokwa looked into Sefakor's face; dazed and was short of words. He looked into the sky and thanked the gods. Impulsively, they both burst into tears of joy.

Apati was overjoyed over what had happened. Spontaneously, the trio busts out singing:

> *We are happy; we are grateful.*
> *God, you have done great things*
> *A great thing you have done for us*
> *A great thing you have done.*

All of them sang together. Abrokwa and Sefakor walked hand in hand and they all left the place and moved towards home with all joy.

Chapter Twenty-Five

Sefakor, Abrokwa and Apati walked for several days before reaching Owle. They spent at least forty days and forty nights on the way. The last night was passed on the outskirts of their village, Owle. Their journey was smooth; unlike the tough one they all had when they were escaping from home.

Before reaching the outskirts of the village, it was already dark. That compelled them to pass the last night on the suburb of Owle. Strategically, they suspended their triumphant entry to the village that evening. They branched to a small deserted farm house and passed the night there on palm branches and plantain leafs.

The following morning, a woman and her daughter woke up early to go and fetch foodstuffs from farm. On the way to farm that dawn, the old woman was narrating Sefakor's story to her daughter. This was a story of the tragic end of a young girl who died prematurely. "This tale was the talk of the village for sometime," she told her daughter.

"This young girl called Sefakor disobeyed her teachers and could not continue her education because of a boy. When punished at school, she took poison and left Owle to take her own life. She never returned until her dry bones were found somewhere in the forest after a year. It was these bones that were brought home and buried," she told her daughter as she paced carefully with her lanky, walking, cassava stick.

The daughter asked series of questions:

"And what happened to her mother? How exactly did Sefakor die?" the girl asked despondently.

"According to the men who fetched her decomposed body, she either killed herself by drinking the poison or was devoured by a wild animal. This incident occurred in the forest you can see in the valley ahead of us. It was only her bones that were brought home and buried after several months," the woman ended.

The woman added that the boys Sefakor was following equally suffered the same fate. Unfortunately for them, nobody located their bodies anywhere to carry home for burial.

As of the time the old woman was telling her daughter this story, Sefakor left home for about six years.

This was the exact time that Abrokwa, Apati and Sefakor woke up and were moving towards home. They wanted to reach home before the crack of dawn.

The girl who had better eye sight saw the people from afar and informed her mother that some young people were coming towards them. "They are carrying small loads. They are three in number. They appear to be a lady and two young men," the girl commented.

The woman who could not see the people clearly because the weather was not clear enough continued with the story until she and her daughter bumped into Abrokwa and his friends. The woman who knew them very well now met them face to face. She got terrified and raised an alarm. This alarm woke up many indigenes from their sleep. The men dashed to the spot of the alarm to curb the unforeseen trouble that was about to befall the village that morning.

Right after the alarm, the woman collapsed and fell into coma. The daughter was taken aback and could not understand why that should happen. When the people reached there, they got shocked to their bones by the sight of Sefakor, Abrokwa and his bosom friend, Apati. These people were pronounced dead several years ago. Yes, the woman saw the ghosts that she was discussing that dawn. Not ordinary ghosts, but perceived accident victims, which should not be met under any circumstance especially at dawn.

Abrokwa and Apati got into action by attending to the collapsed woman. Many people were deeply amazed and some of them rushed back home to report what they saw to other people in the village. Now Tom, Dick and Harry; Mary, Jane and Mercy trooped to the place that early morning to observe for themselves what was perceived to be a miracle. It was no more a matter of someone to hear and come and report to you. Once you are also in the village, you must go and watch.

The friends and relatives of the trio were dumbfounded. Abrokwa and Apati had grown into young handsome men. They had grown beards. Sefakor became a powerful, pretty young lady; more beautiful than how she was before she left Owle.

Convinced that they were not ghosts, the people rushed on them and embraced them with tears of joy.

Sefakor's mother hugged her daughter for several minutes. She sang a lot of joyful songs to thank the gods. Her beloved daughter had returned home alive. Sefakor's younger brother, Daada was overjoyed. He did not know what to do to express his ecstasy. Sefakor's father, Aongo was just shivering when he held Sefakor's hands. He could not work out whether it was a real life event or a dream.

The chief ordered that libation be poured before the three friends entered the village. After the libation, the three were led to the chief's house. That was where they told their stories to the whole village. All and sundry praised Abrokwa and his friend, Apati for a gallant fight. Everybody agreed that, that was true love, therefore, Abrokwa and Sefakor be allowed to marry each other.

A year after their homecoming, a day was set aside for Sefakor and Abrokwa to get married. Like the speed of lightning the day for the marriage ceremony was due. An impressive traditional marriage ceremony was organised for them. The ceremony was heavily attended. Many people from far and near who heard the story wanted to witness the ceremony and they did. It was a type of marriage that was exceptional in the area. The slogan: "Love me to the end. Don't leave me on the way," was displayed in every corner of the village by their peers. Mr Boso, Mr Pataku, the head teacher and the teachers who flogged Sefakor were all invited to witness the grand ceremony. It was a time of joy and reunion but not a time of revenge.

Love Me to the End

At the end of the ceremony everybody present joined Abrokwa and Sefakor and they all sang the song:

> *I chose her for long,*
> *That girl, I chose her for long.*
> *I chose him for long,*
> *That boy, I chose him for long.*
> *The day we shall marry,*
> *The entire community will hear*
> *The day we shall marry,*
> *The entire community will hear.*

From that day, Abrokwa and Sefakor became husband and wife. Apati also had his share of the benefits of the journey. He used the medicine that the dwarfs thought them to heal many sick people in the area. He became a great herbalist at Owle and surrounding towns and villages. He made a lot of money out of his medical work. As good friends as they were, Apati shared some of the proceeds from his business with Abrokwa and his wife, Sefakor. Owing to this, the couple never lacked anything in the marriage.

The end

Thank you for enjoying reading this book. It's available on most online retail shops.
I am eternally grateful to you for leaving a positive feedback on your read.

For Bulk Purchase, please contact:
Archbishop Amissah Memorial School
Box UC 163
University Post Office
Cape Coast
GHANA, West Africa
+233243268937/ +233202321218
justinekor6@gmail.com

About The Author

Justin Ekor was born at Avatime Dzogbefeme in the Volta Region of Ghana. He attended Avatime Secondary School and Amedzofe E.P Training College. After training college, he wrote GCE 'A' levels privately and entered university. He holds a B.Ed. (Hons) and Master of Arts degrees from the University of Cape Coast, Ghana. He is the current headmaster of Archbishop Amissah Memorial Catholic School Cape Coast.

He is a prolific writer with high sense of humour. He enjoys weaving his stories around the culture of his people – the people of Avatime in the Volta region of Ghana in particular and Ewe people in general. Conspicuous in his novels are love and death shrouded in tradition.

He is a songwriter and the writer of the following books:

- *Happy Time Stories for Young Readers*
- *Jolly English for Teenagers.*
- *The Upper Hand in Higher Education.*
- *English Objective Quiz for Junior High Schools*
- *Sex Blindness (Unpublished novel)*
- *Isobobi's Life Journey*
- *Ewegbe Nuti Mor*
- *Nunyaxor me Nutinyawo*